The Silver Gate

THE Silver Gate

KRISTIN BAILEY

KATHERINE TEGEN BOOKS
An Imprint of HarperCollins Publishers

For Tommy and Anna,
because you both are heroes to me

Katherine Tegen Books is an imprint of HarperCollins Publishers.

The Silver Gate

Library of Congress Control Number: 2016935934
ISBN 978-0-06-239857-4

Typography by Aurora Parlagreco
16 17 18 19 20 PC/LSCH 10 9 8 7 6 5 4 3 2 1
❖
First Edition

AUTHOR'S NOTE

I'VE HAD TO THINK A long time about what I should say about Wynn's character. I feel like I'm putting her in a box with very rigid walls if I try to explain her, and I'm not certain that is my role as an author. I set out to create a character readers could love, and I hope she earns that love.

But then I feel I would be doing a disservice to those who are like Wynn if I didn't say something more specific about her. Wynn was born with Rubinstein-Taybi syndrome, a genetic condition that occurs in one of every 125,000 births. Rubinstein-Taybi syndrome is a complicated medical condition that affects those born with it in many different and varying ways. Each person with Rubinstein-Taybi syndrome is an individual with his or her own strengths and weaknesses. In the end, Wynn can be a reflection only of a small part of the broad depth and complexity of this genetic condition.

It can be very difficult to have a condition that is rare. One of the challenging elements of having a rare condition is that few people will have ever heard of it, even doctors. I hope that this story can bring some recognition to rare genetic conditions like Rubinstein-Taybi syndrome. I also hope everyone can see a part of themselves in Wynn. Most of all, I hope you enjoy her adventures.

CHAPTER ONE
Elric

THE RAIN FELL IN HEAVY sheets, lashing Elric's back like the blow of a whip. As he ran, splashes of foul-smelling muck drenched his ankles and soaked through the thin material of his leggings. The mud sucked at his worn shoes and nearly pulled them off.

A light glowed in the distance for only a moment. Elric ran toward it, keeping to the side of the road where the long grasses were slick and beaten down by the storm. If he wasn't careful, he'd slip into the swollen ditch filled with thick black dreck.

Elric pushed forward, keeping an eye on the treacherous ground. The wind picked up, reaching through his worn clothing and chilling his skin. Elric could swear he heard a distant howl in the wind, the triumphant song of a beast intent on harm. The storm had come from nowhere. It had been pleasant all day, but now the wind from the north came in with fury, biting with the harsh cold of the lingering winter.

This was the type of storm that could kill.

He reached the shelter, a crumbling stone church in the center of the village. Really it was nothing more than a pile of rocks with a roof, but it was large and sturdy, and unlikely to blow down in the storm. He knocked, though he could barely hear the sound over the roaring wind. The door opened a crack and Elric hauled the creaking wood with all his strength against the force of the wind, then slipped inside. The door boomed shut behind him.

The hooded man who had opened the door nodded to him, then hunched away toward the front of the church. Half the village huddled around a pitiful fire near the altar while the wind pulled at the thatching on the roof.

"Elric, you survived!" Hereward, the pig-keeper, greeted him with a crooked-toothed smile. He shook out his shaggy hair and droplets of water flew through the air in all directions. "I didn't think you would make it in from the fields. Did you manage to bring the flocks in to safety?"

"No," Elric grumbled. "The storm came on too suddenly and they scattered."

Hereward leaned up against the wall and dug his finger into his ear. He pulled out some wax and looked at it. "Well, that is unlucky. I swear, this is a curse. No village could be this unfortunate. We'll lose half the crop, at least. The newly sown seeds will wash out of the furrows, and your ewes are about to have their lambs." He brushed the wax on the stone wall.

"It's not a curse, it's just rain," Elric grumbled as shook his head to get rid of the water dripping down his neck. "Are the pigs safe?" Hereward was tasked with caring for them, while Elric tended the village's sheep.

Hereward shrugged. "They like mud. They'll survive. That is, if they don't drown." He shivered. "Or freeze."

Elric crossed his arms and rubbed. Now that he was out of the rain, the chill of it sank into his skin, and the smell of damp wool and putrid mud hung on him. "Always one for sunny thoughts, aren't you?"

Hereward stared at Elric as if he had grown another

head. "We are serfs. How could our lives possibly get any worse? We spend all our days and effort tending long strips of fields that don't belong to us. All the fruit of that labor is taken by our lord and master. I tend pigs that I can't eat, and you tend sheep whose wool will never warm us. After our master takes his due, we get to live off of whatever is left. Oh, I forgot. We owe the church a tenth of that. Only then do we eat."

Elric's stomach growled. "I hate this place."

"Careful," Hereward whispered, nodding toward a withered old man in the corner. "Cuthbert is looking sour. Don't give him a reason to spite you."

Old Cuthbert peered over at them, and Elric fidgeted under the man's gaze. He had a sunken socket where his right eye should have been, and a scowl darkened his scarred face. The wound had been punishment for attempting to escape this place. No one from the village ever tried to leave again—especially not with Cuthbert always watching. His failed attempt at a better life made him determined to keep everyone else as miserable as possible. He was all too eager to report any sort of rumblings of dissent to the priest or their lord.

The single-eyed focus on him made Elric feel hot in his face in spite of the cold, so he tucked his chin and wrapped his arms around his legs. He shivered as drops from a leak in the roof hit the floor with a soft and rhythmic *tap, tap, tap.*

"You know," Hereward mumbled, "if we all decided to leave at once, what could Cuthbert do? The lord would finally learn what it takes to plow a field."

"No, our lord will send his soldiers from the garrison to find us all and bring us back. The land has value only if we are here to work on it. They know that. At least they protect us from roaming robbers and thieves." Elric picked a clump of mud off his leggings.

"The soldiers are worse than any thieves in the woods," Hereward grumbled. "The only one with a fouler temper than that lot is the lord himself, but it could be worse. We could work as a slave in the castle and be beaten every day." Hereward mimed being repeatedly struck over the head. "Do you remember poor old Mild? She was sent to work in the kitchens. I saw her at market the other day. She has no teeth left. They've all been knocked out of her head."

Elric didn't know what to say, but ran his tongue over his own teeth, just to be sure they were still there.

Somewhere in the church, a baby cried.

Elric leaned his head back and rolled his eyes. *Get*

used to it, little one. He'd survived thirteen years of this misery, and it wasn't over yet.

The wail of the wretched child filled the church, along with the muffled hushes of its mother.

"Perfect—as if this night couldn't get worse," Hereward groused as the baby continued to screech like a cat caught in a bag. As its cries wore on and on, Elric could see the tension like a rope being pulled tight in the hearts of the others. Something dark seemed to pass over them all. The fires died down, and the shadows grew deeper and more sinister in the corners of the church.

A sour-faced man in a dusty cap winced. A woman with a bulbous nose narrowed her eyes. Their irritated glances met and shared a subtle rage. Finally someone in the church snapped.

"Enough! Quiet that child." Elric couldn't determine who the voice belonged to, but it sounded like a growl. Elric pushed himself up and walked behind the rough wooden benches to get a better view.

A woman and child huddled near the corner by the altar. The baby's face had turned the color of a ripe beet. Elric recognized the mother. Her name was Ailith. She often helped with shearing and carding the wool from the village flock.

"I'm trying!" she said to the wrinkled old man next to her. Elric slipped along the wall until he could see what was happening. Ailith huddled in the corner as if the stone could protect her and her child.

"What sort of mother are you?" grumbled Aebbe, the old woman who lived near the far fields, as she pushed a blanket higher on her shoulders. It made her look like a wrinkled old turtle.

"He's cold and he's hungry, it's natural for him to cry," Ailith said, her limp hair hanging in her face.

"Nonsense," Aebbe said too loudly. The old woman half shouted everything she said, because her hearing had gone. "All God-fearing babes know to be silent in a house of the Lord. Something is not right about this creature. It might be a changeling."

At these words the whole of the church stilled. Other villagers who had been absorbed in their own conversations turned toward the group in the corner. Men and women in the back slowly stood, their necks craning as they peered at the trapped mother and her baby. Slowly people began to press forward.

"Get rid of it before we are all cursed!" a thin man with a sallow face called from the heart of the crowd.

Elric froze. A deeply rooted fear took hold of his gut

and twisted like a knife. He crept forward along the wall, feeling the scrape of stone on his shoulder. His tunic caught on an edge of a stone that had been sloppily stacked in the wall. The mortar crumbled and a piece of rock fell loose. It landed at his feet with a quiet *click*.

"He's not a changeling," Ailith snapped, lifting her son so she could press his little head near the crook of her neck. He continued to fight her, using his tiny fists to push her away. "My baby is not a monster."

Cuthbert had noticed the commotion and stalked across the room. "It does not recognize you as its mother." He pushed past two of the women in the front of the crowd. Elric watched him the way he watched foxes lingering near the edges of his flock. Not even an innocent babe could escape his malice. "Your child was stolen by the fairy folk and they left this wretched thing in its place. It is not human. Look at its twisted face and blotted skin. The only way to force the fairies to bring the true child back is to throw this one in the fire."

"No!" Ailith wrapped her arms tightly around her son, twisting her body as if trying to shield her baby with her own flesh. "My child was not stolen. I have looked over him every moment!" Her voice cracked.

"You took the babe into the woods. I saw you there

only yesterday. You left him sleeping in the grass," Cuth-bert sneered.

"I was gathering wood." Tears streaked down Ail-ith's face.

"It only takes a moment for the fairy folk to steal a child. This storm is your fault. God is punishing us because *you* are keeping a changeling," Cuthbert said. The heavy stillness had returned, like the moment a wolf went still just before it struck. Cuthbert's words hung in the air around them.

Elric felt sick and trapped all at once. He had to do something.

Cuthbert grabbed for the babe.

The mother screamed a high and panicked sound that drowned out the cry of her son.

Without thinking, Elric bent and grabbed the piece of stone that had fallen at his feet. He whipped his wrist and sent the sharp stone flying straight for Cuthbert's thick skull, thankful for the thousands of times he had practiced throwing stones at foxes and wild dogs. It smacked the old troll right on the back of the head.

Cuthbert fell sideways, and it was enough for Ail-ith to wrench her son from his grip and run straight toward Elric along the wall. Others reached for her, but

Elric threw himself into the push of the crowd and away from the wall, giving the mother a narrow gap to run through.

Elbows and shoulders jostled into him as the door of the church opened and slammed shut again. Some of the crowd righted and made for the door, but a clap of thunder stopped their momentum, and the villagers looked to one another as if wondering what they should do now.

Elric watched Cuthbert pick himself up off the ground and touch the back of his head. His palm came away red with blood. "Who threw that rock?" he shouted, a hand pressed to the wound in his greasy hair.

Elric faded into the crowd. He slipped to the far side of the church with his heart pounding in his throat.

"Who cares?" someone grumbled. "Your thick skull can take it, and the crying has stopped."

"What about the changeling?" he demanded. "Fairy children bring ill fortune. Someone has been harboring a wicked creature for years. All the signs have pointed to it. We've found fairy rings amid the crops, and the weather turns without warning. Mark my words. . . ." He pointed his bony finger at the man who had insulted him. "Evil is in our midst. If we don't find it and drive it far from here, it will mean the end of us."

Elric cringed. He refused to believe they were all cursed.

Because if the village was cursed, he knew the reason why.

The men settled around the fire again, muttering about their discomfort.

Hereward pushed through the crowd just as Elric sat on the floor and leaned against the herringbone wall. He took a deep breath and tried to settle his heart. The skin on the back of his neck tingled, and he couldn't fight the urge to twitch his foot.

"You can never leave well enough alone, can you? Nice toss, though," he whispered, settling on the floor cross-legged in front of Elric. "I've been wanting to do that for years. Someone should throw Cuthbert in the fire. If anyone is a curse upon this village, it is him. His face can curdle milk."

Elric gave him a halfhearted chuckle. There was no easy place in this world. He thought about the mother and babe out in the storm, and hoped they could find shelter.

Another wave of thunder rattled and shook the church.

Hereward's younger brother, Osgar, approached, a gangly nine-year-old boy who had too much energy and not enough sense. He reminded Elric of a puppy that couldn't stop wagging its tail. "Do you think God is trying to smite us?" he asked in a gleeful tone, flopping down on the ground beside his brother. "Or perhaps this is the work of the wicked Fairy Queen. I hear she has black wings and sharp teeth, and lightning shoots from her eyes. She must be out there right now."

Elric shook his head in pity. He rubbed his arms, but the goose bumps on his skin didn't go away.

Hereward gave his brother a disgusted look. "What are you, a half-wit?" he asked, then smacked Osgar on the back of the head.

"Don't call him that," Elric said. The muscles in his neck tensed. He hated that term. Nothing made his blood boil faster.

Hereward's thin face twisted in confusion. "Yesterday you called him a fool."

"It's not the same thing."

Osgar looked back and forth between them with wide eyes, as if he wasn't sure what was happening, or if he should feel offended.

Hereward laughed, showing his crooked and rabbity

front teeth. "Half-wit, fool, what does it matter? You don't have a reason to be offended. Even Osgar isn't upset."

Osgar nodded and shrugged. "He calls me a half-wit all the time."

"And he shouldn't," Elric insisted.

"Why not?" Hereward shook out his shaggy hair and pushed it back with his muddy palm.

"Because it's an insult to half-wits," Elric answered. A fool was one thing. A perfectly clever person could choose to act like a fool. Half-wits couldn't help how they were, and it wasn't fair that they were used as the example of a person worthy of scorn. They didn't deserve to be the standard to insult people with no problems at all.

Hereward laughed, his voice ringing against the walls of the church. "That's the funniest thing I've ever—"

Elric shoved him hard.

"What did you do that for?"

"Shut it."

"Do you have a thing for half-wits or something?" Hereward teased with a toothy grin. "Someone would have to be a half-wit to like you."

Elric's fist met Hereward's nose.

And the fight was on. Hereward threw himself forward, tackling Elric and knocking him back against the floor. Elric's head hit the stone, making his ears ring. The grit of the dirty floor slid under his shoulder as he tried to push himself out from beneath the other boy.

Suddenly the church erupted in shouting. Elric gripped Hereward's forearms to keep him from striking. Hereward twisted his arm so he could scratch Elric's face, then yank his hair. Each rip at his skin burned like fire, but he held tight until his hands ached with it. He scrambled his feet against the floor, but the reeds and straw covering the stone slipped out from beneath them. He couldn't get enough traction to push himself free and barely pulled his shoulder out of the way before Hereward bit it.

Hands grabbed at him from all sides as Hereward was ripped away from him. He heard the pig-boy grunt as he hit the floor. The men surrounding him hauled him to his feet as the priest, with his enormous gut, moved into the middle of the fray. He gave Hereward a fierce scowl, then turned a withering look of condemnation toward Elric.

"This is the house of the Lord!" he yelled. "What is the meaning of this?"

"He hit me for no reason!" Hereward shouted, pulling his arm free of the men holding him down and wiping his bloody nose on his sleeve. The motion left a trail of black mud across his cheek and nose. Osgar laughed and pointed, holding his stomach as if his gut would burst with mirth. So much for the loyalty of younger brothers.

Elric forced himself out of the grip of the men holding him and stood. He didn't intend for any of this to be amusing, and yet it was clear what he had said about half-wits didn't matter to either of the brothers. They didn't care who they insulted. They didn't care who they hurt.

The portly priest cleared his throat. "Wrath is a deadly sin," he said. "What would cause you to strike another?"

Elric looked the old priest in the eye as he tried to figure out how a boyish tussle deserved scolding, but threatening to burn a baby alive didn't earn a comment. Thunder clapped overhead as if God himself intended to have his say in the matter.

He couldn't admit why Hereward's words had bothered him as much as they had. She was a secret; he and his father were always so careful to keep her concealed. He knew what would happen if the village at large turned their attention toward her. This night had only proven how deadly the superstitions of the peasants could be. She was innocent, his sister.

A changeling child.

"Forgive me, Father . . . ," Elric mumbled. He touched the back of his hand to his stinging lip, and tasted the filth mingled with his blood.

The priest smiled in his self-important way. "Fear not, my son, you are for—"

"Because I'm not sorry," Elric said. He straightened his cloak and walked out the door, letting it slam behind him. The rain crashed around him, falling in thick sheets that moved across the flooded streets like ghostly waves. He lifted his hood and set out into the darkness.

CHAPTER TWO

Wynn

THE SUN ROSE PINK AND orange in the sky. It was pretty, and the light felt good on Wynn's cheeks. The storm had frightened her, and water dripped through the roof on her all night. The rain nearly put the fire out. The night was so cold.

Mother kept coughing. She needed the fire to keep warm. Wynn had been worried because she wasn't good at starting fires, but she could tend them. She just needed wood. There wasn't much in the house. She had work to do. The storm knocked down many branches in the woods. She could keep the fire hot for Mother with enough sticks. And she was very good at picking up sticks.

"Pick up sticks, pick up sticks," she murmured under her breath as she bent and scrounged on the ground for deadfall. Carefully she placed twigs along behind her, pointing back toward home so she wouldn't lose her way. Mother needed her. She shouldn't get lost. No one would come to find her.

Mother was always so cold now. She didn't really leave her bed anymore, which made Wynn sad. She and Mother had been alone a long time in the woods. Elric said that when he was a baby, he and Mother had lived in the village with Father, but Father and Mother fought when she was born and they had to live apart.

Now Mother lived with Wynn in the woods, and Elric stayed with Father. But Elric liked to visit sometimes, unless he had work in the fields with the sheep. Father didn't visit hardly ever, only when he needed something from Mother's garden. She hadn't seen him in a very long time. That was fine. She wasn't fond of him. He always seemed angry with her and she didn't know why. It didn't matter. She and Mother were alone. She had to make Mother better by herself. The fire would help.

Wynn bunched the group of sticks she had in her hand. Her fingers stretched around them as the prickly bark scratched her palms. She tucked them with the others under a strap of rope so she could carry the large bundle back to the house.

Tightening the rope was difficult with her short, fat thumbs. They never bent quite the right way, but she managed. Mother would be proud of her. Wynn did a good job at finding sticks. It was a task that never frustrated her. Not like the rest of her more difficult chores.

Water dripped off the branches here and there, landing on the wet and slippery leaves on the ground.

"Pick up sticks, pick up sticks," she repeated. She did her best to make the sounds right, the way her brother, Elric, taught her. She always had trouble with making sharp sounds in the back of her throat. Every time she said Elric's name, it sounded more like "Elrith," which rhymed with "Wynnfrith." She liked rhymes. But Elric always corrected her, so she tried to make his name sound the right way. She liked it when he said she did a good job speaking.

Her mother said she had trouble learning because she could speak the fairy tongue, and had trouble with the human one. Wynn didn't know if that was true. She tried to speak with the fairies, but she couldn't see them, and they didn't answer back.

A loud caw broke the peaceful quiet of the morning. The sound startled Wynn, and she looked up.

A raven sat on a branch only an arm's length from her face. Oh, he was handsome, with coal-black feathers. They shined in the morning sunlight. He cocked his head to the side in the way birds sometimes did. Wynn mimicked his motion, wondering why he liked to look at things sideways.

Caw! The raven called again, and shook out his wings. His shoulders hitched up, turning his feathers into a spiky crest. His call repeated, as if the wind had become taken with the sound. Maybe he liked to practice his sounds too.

Wings fluttered behind her.

Wynn turned.

Two more ravens landed. The bare branches rattled as the birds flapped and settled in the tree. A shower of drops fell over her, feeling cold on her head and neck. A twig broke off and landed at her feet. Wynn bent and picked it up. A sharp sliver poked into her wide and stunted thumb. She dropped the stick quickly.

Another raven came, and another.

Wynn looked around the scattered grove. A large cluster of ravens joined the others in the tree. She tried to count them, but she made it only to thirteen before more came too quickly. She had never seen so many before.

In the distance she could see her home through the bare branches of the wood. The tiny mud-walled hut hid behind the dead plants that the winter had killed in the garden.

No smoke rose from the thatched roof.

Oh no.

The fire had gone out!

Wynn ran as fast as she could, brambles and wet leaves slapping at her ankles. She could feel every sharp rock against the thin soles of her shoes, but she didn't stop. Sticks came loose from her rope and fell against the backs of her legs and heels as she ran.

The ravens took flight and swooped close over her head, catching the wind as they dipped low. They flapped their wings with a sound like a roar and collected on the roof, a storm of black wings and sharp beaks. They cawed. The sound filled the woods.

Wynn could feel it in her tummy. There was danger here.

Her heart stuttered and skipped, and her tongue felt

thick and dry. She came to the broken gate. Elric needed to fix it, but he hadn't come in a very long time. Wynn yanked hard on the gate, but it wouldn't budge. The fence was short, sticks buried in the ground and woven together with rope to keep rabbits out. But the sharp ends of the sticks pointed up.

Wynn tried to straddle the fence, but the point of a stick caught under the long skirt of her kirtle dress and scratched her leg. She tumbled over the top, landing hard on the cold, wet ground of the garden and pulling down half the fence. The chickens scattered. Wynn picked herself up and ran to the door.

The ravens on the roof watched her with their shining eyes. They didn't pick at the thatching the way they usually did. She crept in through the open doorway. Her rope strap for her stick bundle had come undone and only two of her sticks remained, tangled in the braided fibers. She dropped the old rope near the door.

"Modder?" Wynn called, hating that the word came out so wrong. She didn't have time to think about it. The small fire had gone out. A chill lingered in the air. The morning sunlight slanted through the door and fell across her mother's face.

Her mother's eyes stared toward the door, one hand

falling limply over the edge of the bed. A fly landed on her mother's cheek, crawling toward her eye.

Wynn stood motionless in the doorway as the ravens cried and cried.

Danger.

Wynn took hesitant steps across the small hut. A gust of wind blew in from the door, scattering pale ashes across the hearthstone.

"I'm sorry, Mother," she whispered as she sat on the edge of the blanket covering the crinkling hay. She tried to hold her mother's hand, but it was cold. Her fingers didn't curl around Wynn's palm the way they always had. "The fire went out. I didn't bring your sticks."

Wynn sat for a long time with her hand on her mother's knee and listened to the ravens. She let the tears fall over her cheeks because she didn't know what else to do. She let them fall because she loved her mother. She let them fall because she was cold and scared. She let them fall because she'd never been so alone.

Lifting her head, she wiped her nose on her sleeve and looked around. She couldn't stay in the house with her dead mother through the night. She had to do something. She needed to find her brother before it turned dark and she had no fire. Elric would know what to do.

Wynn left the house. The chickens scratched in the yard. They didn't listen to the ravens. Her body felt heavy and sick. Her favorite black hen trotted at her heels, but stopped when she pushed hard on the gate. It broke off the fence and collapsed on the path.

Elric would fix it.

Wynn's stomach rumbled as she followed the path that Elric always took when he left. If she followed it long enough, she would find him. She hadn't eaten, but with the ill feeling in her middle, she didn't want to.

The woods thinned out to large open patches of brown mud that stretched over the hills. A big garden could grow there. Wynn's garden was little.

A scary-looking man with only one eye stared at her as she passed on the muddy path. She kept her eyes down and didn't speak, just as her mother told her. She wasn't ever supposed to look at or speak to anyone if they ever came near the hut. She was supposed to hide. She pulled her long braid over her shoulder, then hunched, hoping the man wouldn't speak to her, because then she would have to say something and he would know she didn't say her words right.

Wynn had never been here and it made her feel

scared. Elric told her never to leave the woods, that the people of the village weren't nice. She believed Elric, because he never lied to her.

Maybe she didn't have to speak *to* anyone to find her brother. "Elric?" she called, hoping he would hear her. "Elric?"

A woman in a dark dress passed by, patting the back of a wiggly baby. Wynn smiled at the baby. He laughed at her.

"Hello," the woman said. She looked pale and tired. Or maybe she'd been crying. Her eyes were red.

Wynn blinked at her, then looked at the skirt of her own long kirtle.

"Are you looking for something?" she asked.

Wynn nodded. "Elric," she said.

"Who is Elrith?" The woman tipped her head and looked at her the way Mother had when she couldn't understand Wynn's words.

Wynn took a deep breath. "El . . . rit." It sounded better, but it still wasn't right, and Wynn knew it. She hated that her mouth wouldn't form the sound.

"Oh, do you mean Elric?" the woman asked, shifting the baby to her other hip.

"Yes!" Wynn smiled at her, hopeful for the first time.

Elric was wrong. The people in the village were very nice.

"My sister said he's been sent afield to gather the animals that ran off in the storm. He won't return for days yet. If you see him, can you tell him that Ailith is grateful to him? He'll know why." She hugged her baby very tightly.

Wynn nodded, but she didn't think she would remember. She would try, though.

The woman continued on with her baby, walking down the path. The baby smiled at Wynn from over the woman's shoulder. Wynn's heart sank as she watched the woman disappear. Elric was gone with the sheep and couldn't help her.

Something grabbed her elbow. She froze as a man turned her around.

"Wynnfrith, what are you doing here?" Her father's face was red, which made the scar down his cheek look even scarier. His shaggy barley-colored hair fell into his eyes as he glared at her. His voice sounded angry, and he was so big. She was supposed to stay away from him. Mother told her never to cross him, and he was cross now. "You know you're not supposed to be here."

Her words wouldn't come. Her mind was moving slowly again. She couldn't make her mouth move right. She blinked as tears formed in her eyes.

"Where is your mother?" He tightened his grip on her elbow and dragged her back along the road toward the woods, sending pain up her arm. "She swore she would keep you hidden away. That was our bargain when I let her keep you."

Her father hurt her as he dragged her along the path, but she couldn't say anything, and she was afraid to make him more angry if she did. He hated the way she spoke. The few times he had come to the hut, he didn't even look at her. "I should have forced her to return to me," he muttered under his breath. "She is still my wife. Make no mistake. Perhaps it is time for our arrangement to change."

Wynn stumbled as he dragged her. His legs were long and hers were not. She couldn't keep her feet under her. When she tripped on her hem, he yanked her back up, pulling her shoulder so hard she cried out.

Once he reached the garden, he let go, and Wynn collapsed in the dried-out husks of the old pumpkin vine and rubbed her sore elbow. He violently pushed open the door. "Hild!" he shouted, then he fell still. "Hild?"

He entered the hut slowly. Wynn followed him to the door and watched as he knelt next to her mother and took her limp hand in his. He kissed the back of it and reached out to close her eyes.

"When did this happen?" he asked, his voice very different than it had been.

Wynn couldn't say anything.

"Answer me!" he shouted.

Wynn took a step back. "The storm."

He looked down and nodded his head. "You've grown since the last time I saw you. How old are you now?"

She swallowed, her mind searching for the right answer. Thankfully he waited without yelling at her. "I . . . am . . . eleven," she whispered.

She didn't want to live with her father. She wanted to stay here in her hut with her chickens. Elric could help her. She would be good. She would never go toward the village again.

Her father lifted her mother in his arms and carried her to the door. It almost looked as if Mother was sleeping.

"I'll take care of this," her father said. His mouth set in a grim line as he strode back through the door, forcing Wynn to move away as if she wasn't really there. "I should have taken care of things long ago."

CHAPTER THREE

Elric

ELRIC WHISTLED TO THE FLOCK as he drove them down the muddy road. Over the past few days, the entire hamlet had been busy with repairs to the houses and digging mud out of homes near the bottom of the hill. He hadn't been digging mud out of houses, but he looked as if he had. He'd climbed through endless soggy fields and swollen creeks in his search for all the lost sheep. Now mud caked on his legs so thick, his feet looked like the trunks of gnarled trees.

It had taken him four days to gather the animals

through briars and bogs, and all he wanted now was to curl up on a dry bed of straw and sleep for a week. At least the solitude of the countryside was pleasant and he didn't have to hear his father's complaints about tending the land assigned to him by their lord. Still, he was hungry, tired, thirsty, and in a foul mood as he used a stick to drive the filthy sheep back toward the village.

Thankfully he'd recovered nearly the whole flock. Two of the sheep had been mauled by wild dogs. One had broken a leg and drowned in the swollen creek. The others looked grimy, but healthy. He didn't envy Ailith, who would have to clean the wool. Maybe that was a task he could teach Wynn to do. He'd have to show her next time he found a free day to visit her and Mother. He hadn't seen them in several weeks. Elric picked up his pace. The fallow fields where the animals could graze weren't far.

A strange feeling crept over Elric's neck, and he glanced behind him. A man followed him. In the glare of the late afternoon, Elric didn't recognize him at first. Squinting, he realized who it was and immediately wished he could turn and walk the other way. There was no mistaking the way his father hunched his shoulders, or the hitch in his step as he walked.

"Elric!" he called, raising his hand. "Son!"

Elric stopped and stiffened. He had no choice now but to wait for his father to reach him.

"What a fortune meeting you on the road like this," he said, short of breath. It was strange. Elric couldn't imagine what his father was doing so far from the village. Surely the others needed his skill to replace the damaged thatching on the roofs after such a powerful storm.

His father squinted into the sun, the skin around his eyes wrinkling deeply.

Elric wondered if he would look as worn as his father when he grew older. They shared a lanky build, light brown hair and wide mouth, but his father had a sunken eyes, a hollow look to his cheeks, and an ugly scar across his face. It began near the bridge of his nose, dangerously close to his eye, and crossed his cheek until it touched his ear—a gift from their lord when he had been a boy. His father was lucky he had only one horrible scar, at least on his flesh. His mind carried far more.

Whatever Elric's father wanted, he'd say it soon enough. He'd always been a blunt man. Today he had a grave look on his face. "I've just been to see our lord," he said. "I have it all arranged."

Elric backed up a step. "What are you talking about?" Yes, they were all sworn to lord and land, and forced to work to pay their tribute or face the ugly consequences. But unless enemy soldiers were sacking the village, there was little reason to seek out the attention of the castle. In Elric's opinion, staying far away from that place was a good idea.

"You haven't heard?" His father looked genuinely perplexed, as if he suddenly didn't know what he should say. That was a rare thing.

"Heard what?" Elric was growing frustrated.

"Your mother is dead," his father said. "I buried her three days ago, poor soul."

Elric didn't hear the words. He felt them. They stabbed deep, like sharpened pikes aimed at his heart and piercing through his stomach. His mother, dead? She couldn't be gone. She was too strong. She had managed to live in the woods in secret and raise Wynn on her own, which was a miracle.

Elric's father placed a hand on his shoulder, as if that gesture could take away the shock and the pain inflicted by his words. "It's a terrible pity, and I'm sorry. I was quite fond of Hild in her youth, before, well—" He scratched his head. "Before everything went so very wrong between us. Still, she was my wife, and I kept her secrets. I was loyal to her. I don't want you to forget that. And now you don't have to worry. Everything is taken care of."

A second wave of dread washed over Elric, pulling him out of his shock. "What is?"

"The changeling, of course," his father said. "I have sold her. Perhaps now good fortune might return to this place."

Elric's father clapped him across the back, signaling the end of the conversation.

Wynn.

"You sold her?" His mind raced through all the terrifying possibilities.

His father's expression turned hard, the way it always did when Elric questioned his wishes. "I struck a bargain. She'll change the straw and reeds on the floor of the lord's castle. She can keep the scraps she finds under the tables and sleep on the floor of the kitchens." He contorted his face into a weak grin to cover his discomfort. "It's a simple task, one she can manage without a problem. Since she looks normal enough, they shouldn't suspect what she is as long as she doesn't speak. She won't be a burden and she'll have a place to live."

Elric's throat tightened. "She'll be treated like a dog!" She'd have to scrounge for leftover bones beneath tables, like she wasn't even human. On top of that, their lord was cruel. The thought of Wynn in that place, being beaten until she lost all her teeth, filled his mind until he could no longer spare a thought for his own dead mother. "How can you do this? She's my sister!" Elric's heart beat fast and hard in his chest.

His father sighed. They had been having this conversation since Elric was small.

"She's not your sister," he insisted. "She's a changeling, and she's not of our blood. Your true sister was stolen as an infant by the Fairy Queen and never returned. I mourned that child long ago, as you should have. The creature they left in your sister's place is not of us. God doesn't make such mistakes."

"Changeling or no," Elric said, his voice cracking, "she's completely innocent."

His father's gaze tilted up to the heavens, then dropped back to settle on Elric in anger. "If she were innocent, she wouldn't be afflicted. Vanity caused this curse. Your mother was too proud to have a daughter, proud of all the dark hair the babe was born with. Of course the fairies would notice the child and covet it.

That's why your real sister was stolen."

"That's not true," Elric said.

"You want the truth? I'll tell you what really happened, all the things your mother never wanted you to know. I begged her to get rid of the changeling before anyone became attached to it, but Hild was stubborn. So I took the babe out in the woods in the middle of a snowstorm in the hopes that it would mercifully freeze to death. It was the kind thing to do. When your mother discovered the changeling missing, she ran out into the woods in the middle of the night. I don't know what foul magic led your mother to the creature, but she found it and brought it back. That's when I knew for certain what she was. Only unholy magic could have kept a baby alive alone in that snow."

Elric stared at his father, speechless and appalled. His whole body chilled, as if he were lost in the snowy woods too. "When your mother returned to the house, it was only to pack her things. She said she was leaving, and there was nothing I could do about it. She said if I didn't let her go, I'd never see you again. You! You're my *son*, Elric. You're the only good thing I have. I couldn't let you go, so I let her leave and take the creature with her. I figured the changeling would die within a month or two and she'd be back. Instead your mother built her hut, planted her garden, and raised that unnatural child alone. It is a mark of my patience that I helped at all, that I'm helping now."

Elric squared his shoulders, standing to nearly his father's height. "Why can't you just let her be? I'll take care of her."

·His father's eyebrows rose, as if the thought had never occurred to him. "You're only a boy, not yet fourteen. You have responsibilities in the village. Who will look after the flock? One day my bond to our lord will be yours and you will have to plow the fields allotted to me. They are good fields. They are some of the most bountiful, if tended correctly. They will give you enough for you to feed your own family and carry on. That is the life you were born to have, not caring for a half-wit sister who is of no use to anyone." His tone left no room for argument. Elric bristled.

"We cannot disappoint our lord," Elric's father said, his voice quieter. "I can't afford to feed her, especially— not after this storm. And should we not give our due in tithe and taxes, we'll suffer much worse than this." He ran his finger over his scar. "At the castle, the girl will have food. She'll have a warm place to sleep near the fire. I'm doing her a kindness, really." Elric's father reached out and placed a hand on Elric's head. He let it slide down and cupped the back of Elric's neck. "Don't worry. She's pitiful enough. They won't beat her badly."

Elric shrugged away from his touch. "She won't understand."

His father turned and began walking through the loosely scattered sheep. "Perhaps that is a blessing."

Elric watched him walk away and felt a dread he had never known as his father strode toward the village, and closer to Wynn. His father never dallied about with anything. If he had made a decision, he'd see it done and quickly. Elric had to find her.

Yes, by everyone's account Wynn was afflicted, but in truth she was kind, loving, and funny. She was human. She didn't deserve this fate. No one deserved this. He couldn't allow her to be tortured and abused for the rest of her life.

He was Wynn's brother, changeling or no. And now he needed to protect her.

He knew all too well no one else would.

Elric glanced back at the sheep. They were close to the village now. Surely the other villagers would find the flock. The sheep wouldn't wander far. He had to reach Wynn before his father did.

With his father following the road toward the village, Elric veered to the right and took off running across the countryside toward a shortcut he'd used before. The sheep spread out around the road, happily grazing as he ran through a muddy barley field.

The new grasses of the crop had been beaten into the mud by the storm. He struggled over the furrows in the soggy dirt until he reached the edge of a wood that stretched beyond imagining.

He'd never make it in time. And Wynn would follow their father like a lamb to the slaughter.

Elric raced as if the devil himself had come for him. The woods were unkind, lashing at him with fallen branches, patches of thorny brambles, and ditches swollen with water.

At last he saw his mother's hut through the trees. His throat burned as he panted for breath. Sweat dripped down the sides of his face. He launched himself over the broken front gate and charged through the dead garden.

He burst in through his mother's door.

No one was there but a fat black hen pecking at the floor.

CHAPTER FOUR
Elric

COLD ASHES SCATTERED ACROSS THE hearthstone
and into the reeds. The dark spotted chicken let out
low guttural clucks as it searched for ticks to eat. Each
scratch of its claws on the hard dirt floor sent a chill
down Elric's spine. The lingering sweet smell of death
twisted through his stomach, and his heart raced.

He had been living for too long in the village and
out in the fields. He didn't know the hut had gotten so
bad. A bucket of filthy water festered in the corner with
blood-soaked rags, a muddy, hole-ridden dress lying in a

pile beside it. A large piece of Mother's favorite clay bowl had broken off, leaving a jagged edge and a long crack down the side. Straw on the floor clumped together like a molding black rug. The neglect crushed something inside of him. He pictured his ailing mother lying on the bed. He couldn't reconcile the image with her round face and laughing eyes. She'd always had a smile for him. Sometimes it was wide and open, as broad and warm as the love he held for her. Other times it was quiet, a hidden game between them. He would try to make her laugh, and she would pretend not to notice his antics. A slight smile that only turned up the corners of her lips always gave her away.

"What are you doing with my spoon?" she asked him, in a memory that felt as far away as the stars.

"It is not a spoon, it is my sword. I am a knight on a quest." He swung his "sword" through the air in mock combat.

"And what sort of quest is this?" She wiped her hands on a rag before placing them on her hips. The smile was there, softly hidden behind the affection in her eyes.

"The bravest and most dangerous kind—a quest to the Silver Gate!" he said. Suddenly Wynn tumbled in through the door, tripping on her feet because she couldn't walk well

yet. She laughed as one of the chickens pecked at the folds of her skirt. She tried to hug it, but the bird ran out through the door. "Mmmmnnn!" Wynn shouted after the hen. She pushed herself up and chased after it, her arms spread wide.

Elric brandished his sword once more. "I took Wynn to the Silver Gate with me. We passed the fire and found a pond and a fairy ring in the woods. But the terrible monster Grendel chased us home. Do you have a new quest for us?" he asked.

His mother laughed as she caught the "sword" mid-swing, then picked him up in a warm embrace and kissed him on the forehead. "Just take care of your sister. Stay with her. Keep her safe for me. Will you, my brave knight?"

Elric nodded.

She put him down and ruffled his hair. "Good, now go forth on the dangerous quest to find me the perfect onion for the soup."

Elric picked up the wooden spoon at his feet, the one he had used as that great sword, then tucked it into his belt. All that lingered in this place was the specter of death. His mother was gone. He couldn't leave his sister here.

"Wynn!" he called out the window, hoping she was near the garden.

The chicken picked up its head and bolted away from him. It fluttered into the window and clucked in protest as he left the house.

He sucked in a deep breath of fresh air. A cold wind blew his hair so it brushed against his neck. Wynn couldn't be gone. He had run, and Father had been walking toward the village. His journey would take three times as long if he stayed on the paths going up the hill to the village and then back down into the woods. Cutting through the woods had given him time, but not much. Where was she?

"Wynn!" he called again as he ruthlessly trampled over the remains of his mother's precious herbs and back into the woods beyond. He skidded down a muddy slope as he called his sister's name.

The thick curling branches of the old oaks hovered over him as the acorns and dried leaves crunched beneath his worn boots. It was a place of twisting shadows and eerie silence. That's when he heard it, the whisper of a familiar song. He could swear he could hear several soft voices in harmony blending with the lilting tones of a wooden pipe and the low thump of drums. Particles of dust floated through the light and shadows beneath the trees. They seemed to dance to the hidden music.

He had to concentrate to hear it. It was faint, as if the melody were crossing a great distance on the wind. A tingle crept over his skin, like cobwebs brushing over the hairs on his arms and neck. He turned toward the meadow to his left and ran toward the bright area beyond the thick trunks of the trees.

Wynn!

A distance away, she knelt by a lonely pile of rocks that covered a freshly dug grave. She placed sprigs of flowers and common meadow weeds on the stones.

The melody continued, but it was only his sister singing in her sweet but off-tune voice. Strange. It had sounded like so many voices, singing in harmony.

He recognized the tune right away. It wasn't a church hymn, but a lullaby their mother used to sing late at night when she thought they were sleeping. It told of a journey to the Silver Gate, where the Fairy Queen would welcome them home.

"Wynn?" he called. He was so relieved to see her, but he hadn't yet recovered from the shock of all his father had told him, and now the finality of his mother's death hit him as he stared at her grave.

His sister turned to him and immediately smiled, as if her entire world hadn't just crumbled. Though her eyes always looked hooded and downturned, there was no hiding the excitement in them as she pushed to her feet and ran to him with her arms flung wide.

He folded her into a tight hug as she buried her face against his chest. They didn't say anything as they held each other.

"Elric," Wynn said against his tunic. "Mother is gone."

"I know."

There was nothing Elric could do to change his mother's fate. She had only once ever asked anything of him. He swore he would keep that promise now. He would keep his sister safe.

"What do we do?" she asked.

He put his hands on her shoulders and pushed her back so he could look her in the eye. "We're going to go away from here, just you and me."

"No," she said, shaking her head. "We can't. It's not allowed."

He let go of her shoulders and took one of her hands, but she didn't grip his back. "We must. It's not safe to stay here."

She looked at him as if he had gone mad. "The house is safe," Wynn said, dragging her feet as he tried to pull her forward. "We can fix the roof with bark. You can stay with me now. I can feed the chickens. You can start the fire. I'll bring you sticks."

She forced the words out with as clear sounds as she could manage.

He gave her arm a tug. "We can't stay at the house. Father is coming to take you away." They didn't have time to linger. They needed food, a knife, clothes, cloaks. How was he to manage this? He was running out of time.

"Father doesn't like me. He told me to hide in the hut and don't come out until he gets back. I didn't listen." Her brow furrowed.

Elric had to act fast. They didn't have much time, and he didn't know how to get her to follow . . .

Wait. Yes, he did know. "I know what we should do. Let's go on an adventure. The way we did when we were little." He forced himself to sound excited.

Her face eased back into its usual sweet expression. "To find the Silver Gate?" she asked.

"That's right," he said, remembering the game they used to play on summer days. They'd wander through the woods in search of the court of the Fairy Queen. "We'll find the Silver Gate this time. Just follow where I lead."

He reached out his hand. She looked at it, and her head cocked to the side the way a suspicious fox does when it isn't sure if it should take the next step into the open. His hand began to tremble as he held it out. Finally, she placed her hand in his.

Relief rushed through Elric. One day, she might be able to understand that all he wanted was to save her. He hoped she'd know. But there was no time for the truth. Their father was coming, and if he didn't act now, it would be too late.

CHAPTER FIVE
Elric

ELRIC BURST THROUGH THE DOOR of their mother's hut, pulling Wynn behind him. The hens scattered with a flurry of flapping wings and agitated clucks. Wynn let go of his hand and chased one toward the window while he rummaged through a box in the corner.

He grabbed a sack and then tossed one to Wynn just as the hen escaped her grasp. The sack landed on her arm and hung there. "Don't worry about the chickens," Elric insisted. "They'll fatten themselves on caterpillars in the garden. We have to go, and quickly. Take anything you think we might need."

"I'll do a good job," she said, then ran outside. It probably wasn't wise to leave the packing to her. For all he knew, she'd pack something heavy and useless, like a stool. But giving her a task would keep her busy as he filled his own sack: flint, clothes, knife, food.

With his sack full, he stepped out into the garden just as their father turned the bend at the end of the path. He was walking toward the hut.

Elric dashed around the side of the hut with his heart caught in his throat. He couldn't tell if his father had seen him. Looking back over one shoulder, he crept along the side of the house and almost collided with Wynn. He had to catch her as she stumbled backward.

"C'mon," he whispered. He grabbed her hand and led her through the garden to the back gate. "Hurry, we have to sneak past the Grendel."

Wynn's face lit up at his words. He started running, pulling her along. Wynn followed as quickly as she could.

It wasn't fast enough.

Elric dodged through the thick trees, grasping her arm to help her balance as she ran. Turning away from the meadow, he led them toward the thickest part of the woods, but the trees were old and well spaced. Father would still be able to see them.

"Down here," Elric whispered to Wynn. He followed the slope of a hill toward a growing thicket where rainwater flowed down the hill and into a small gulley. The woods grew darker and the leaves crunched beneath their feet. Elric jumped over the small creek and then reached back for Wynn.

There was a loud shout in the distance.

Father's silhouette appeared at the top of the hill.

Wynn stiffened. "Is that the Grendel?" Her eyes were wide with fear.

"Yes." He wished it was. The Grendel was the least of their problems. "He's coming. Quickly, jump!"

Wynn swung her arms forward as if to jump, but then caught herself and kept her feet firmly planted on the bank.

"We don't have time, just jump!" he called. She reached one hand out to his, but he couldn't quite reach it. Their fingertips brushed and again she leaned back, unable to jump.

"I'll catch you." He held his arms out to her. She screwed her lips into a tight frown, swung her arms, and jumped off the bank, though she half stopped herself mid-jump and fell forward.

Elric grabbed her and threw his weight back. He managed to pull her across the creek, but they stumbled and fell on the bank.

"Oh, we made it!" Wynn exclaimed triumphantly. Elric hushed her as he pulled her up and they ran toward the thick brush. It was no use. They'd never get away like this.

Their father started down the hill. They had to hide before he spotted them. A dense thicket of blackthorn grew beneath a newly fallen tree. Elric paused. The rounded leaves had turned yellow and thinned out, exposing the wicked thorns. They were easily the length of a babe's finger.

"Cover your face with your cloak," Elric said, lifting Wynn's hood over her head, then grabbing his own. "We have to hide."

Wynn balked and pulled her hand from his. "Blackthorn is danger," Wynn said.

The blackthorn was thick, and if they could tuck themselves behind the fallen tree, they'd be well concealed. His father would never think to look for them in that tangle of thorns. "It will protect us," he whispered. "Trust me." His heart raced. Blackthorn could be dangerous. Scratches could easily fester. He was about to hide beneath the hedgerow of the devil, but they had no choice. Father would reach the creek soon. He shouted their names as he tromped through the crunching leaves.

Hunching his shoulders, Elric crouched low and backed into the thicket. The rotting sloe berries squished beneath his feet as he tried to keep Wynn's face protected. He could feel the thorns jabbing into his back through the thick wool of his clothing.

The thorns caught and pulled at his sleeves and his sack, sharp claws intent on a blood tribute for daring to seek their shelter. Elric pushed on. Once they were behind the fallen log, he tucked Wynn under his arm and pulled her cloak to conceal her. Thankfully their cloaks were mottled gray and blended into the shadows of the thicket.

Elric's fear grew until it became a monster within his own mind. The same oppressive feeling he'd noticed at the church came over him, as if they were being watched—as if something powerful wanted them to be found. He could feel the heavy air all around them, the thousand needlelike jabs waiting to rip at his flesh. Now they had no way to run.

He peeked out from under his hood, trying not to move a muscle.

"Will the Grendel eat us?" Wynn whispered.

"Yes," Elric whispered back as Wynn shook beneath his arm. "Quiet now, or he will find us."

He held Wynn tightly, almost as tightly as he held his own breath.

Please stay still, please stay still, please stay still.

Their father was close.

"Wynnfrith?" their father's rasping voice called, as if he had run after them. "It's your father. It's your duty to obey me."

Wynn stiffened under Elric's arm. He gripped her shoulder, hoping to keep her down. He brought her closer to his chest so he could reach around and cover her mouth if he had to, but thankfully, she stayed silent.

Their father moved harshly through the brush, and Elric hoped he would just keep going, but the crunching of his boots on the deadfall stopped after only five paces.

"Elric?" he called. "I saw you run." *Crunch, crunch,* he paced away. *Crunch, crunch, snap.* He came closer again. He stilled, as if he were listening for them. "Come back home. You are no fool, you know what punishment could come to you."

Wynn struggled, and Elric hugged his sister tighter.

Elric's neck hurt from their hunching and his toes began to go numb. But their father wouldn't leave. Once again, he circled back toward the blackthorn. It was almost as if he knew where they were. Elric could see the rough seam of his father's shoe from the narrow gap beneath the log.

A low-throated *awwwwwwwwwwwwwww* sounded from somewhere next to Wynn.

Elric froze in shock. That couldn't be what he thought it was. Their father's shoe edged closer.

The grove fell silent.

Something moved against Elric's ankle. He looked down at the sack Wynn had packed. The coarsely woven cloth jabbed outward with a low *cluck, cluck, awwwwwwwwwwww.*

She'd packed a chicken!

The blackthorn rustled to their left. Father was still out there.

Elric grabbed the sack and yanked it up, but Wynn clung to it. Slapping off her hands, he tugged at the leather tie and the sack flew open.

A fat black hen burst out, darted through the thorny branches with her wings thrown forward, and ducked under the log.

Elric covered Wynn's mouth and tightened his hold on her as she struggled forward after her hen.

The hen squawked and their father let out a shout.

Elric listened as the hen's quick feet dashed through the leaves, and her throaty call hung in the air as she raced away. Something wet leaked under his palm. Tears. Wynn was crying.

"God's bones," their father cursed. Elric heard the loud crack of their father hitting the trunk of a tree with a branch. His footsteps crunched across the glade, growing more and more distant. Their father's rough voice called out into the empty woods.

"Wynnfrith! Elric!" The voice faded as the stillness of the woods descended. "Wynn . . ." And then there was nothing.

Elric waited.

Wynn struggled and pulled against his hold, but he held her tight and waited. He waited until his thighs shook from fatigue and his feet lost all feeling. His shoulders ached. His neck ached. The thorns bit at his skin, but he waited.

One wrong move, and it meant Wynn's life. Father would forgive him. For as surly as their father could be, he valued his only son. He would give some excuse to the villagers about Elric going after another stray sheep should they question his delay. Elric would be fine. It was his sister he was worried about. She would pay the price for all of this.

Minutes passed like hours. Finally, when Wynn stopped struggling and the shadows began to stretch, he loosened his hold. She wormed her way under the log and out of the thicket.

A thousand thorns stabbed at him as he pushed out from the tangled bush.

He touched his knuckle against his cheek, and it came away smeared with blood.

Across the way, Wynn had made it back to the creek. She bent as if she wanted to jump, but she didn't have the courage to make the leap across the gully on her own. He hurried to catch up with her, in spite of the numbness in his feet.

He grabbed her by the shoulder and turned her around.

"You packed a *chicken* in your sack?" He would have asked what she was thinking, but he knew what she was thinking.

She pulled her arm away from him with a hard yank. The motion threw his balance forward and he almost fell into the gully. Sometimes he forgot how strong she could be.

"Mildred is my favorite." Wynn wiped her nose on the back of her hand.

"Wynn, you can't bring a chicken." His feet stung from falling asleep, and his cheek stung too from the wound. The last thing he needed was for it to fester, but he couldn't treat it now. This journey was off to a terrible start, and they hadn't even left their mother's woods.

"We brought a chicken to the Gate before," she reasoned, harkening back to their childhood games.

"Wynn, we aren't going to some ring of rocks in the woods. We have to go far away from here, and a chicken will only get in the way." He wasn't quite sure where to go yet. His only thought had been to get away from their father. Now that he was faced with the uncertainty of where to go next, he felt uneasy. He had to find a place that would be safe for her. "What else did you put in here?" He rummaged through her sack. It was full of uprooted weeds, a pot, and a small jar of honey nestled in the middle. "Weeds and honey. That's what you chose to bring. The only useful thing you packed was the pot."

"I like honey. We can eat some at the fairy ring. You said this is a game." She glared at him, and Elric felt the weight of her anger. "You lied." She snatched her sack away from him.

"I'm sorry." It was all he could say.

Wynn crossed her arms over her chest. She swayed the way she used to when she was small. "Father will hurt me?" Her words came out haltingly, as if her thoughts couldn't quite put the lot of them together.

Elric wasn't sure what to say. He wished they could go back in time and be children again.

"He doesn't want to hurt you. He just wants to be rid of you." The words almost made him ill, but they were the truth, and he couldn't hide them from her. She was in danger, and she needed to know it.

Wynn might have trouble, but she wasn't what they said she was. She could think. Every once in a while, she understood too well what was going on. He hoped now was one of those moments.

He needed her to understand him now.

"Why doesn't he like me?" She looked up at him with her downturned eyes. They matched the color of the clear autumn sky.

Elric didn't know what to say. He knew the answer, but he couldn't bring himself to say those words. "I don't know," Elric lied.

Wynn turned away from him with her arms still crossed and started walking through the glade away from the hut and the village. He trotted up next to her and reached out to ruffle her hair. She pulled her head away, but stopped walking and looked up at him. "I like you," he said. That was not a lie.

Her lips pressed together as she considered their situation. "Where do we go?" she asked.

That was a good question. Once Father brought him an apple. He'd said he traded with some nuns for it at a convent to the north. Maybe Wynn could find a home there.

Elric held out a hand. "Just follow me. I'll keep you safe." A rumor of a convent somewhere to the north was very little to go on, but it was as good a direction as any. He just hoped she wouldn't notice that he had no real plan.

"Keep you safe?" she asked, repeating his words exactly. It was an old habit she fell back on when she was scared. He hated seeing her afraid.

"I'm going to take you to a place with high walls and kind women who will let you care for the chickens," he said. He didn't know if that was true, but there was little other comfort he could give his sister, and it was his deepest hope that it might be true.

She needed to trust him.

"Will I have to start the fires?" she asked.

"Never," he said. Hoped.

Wynn reached out and placed her hand in his. Elric gripped it as they walked under the shade of the oaks.

It was up to him now.

CHAPTER SIX

Elric

"COME ON, WYNN. LET'S GO this way." Elric glanced up at the sun through the thick branches above. It was the first day it had shone brightly since the storm. The clouds looked like piles of soft, clean wool in the vivid blue sky. He welcomed the sun, not only as an end to the storm, but also to give him a sense of direction. It was already tilting westerly, and they didn't have much time until nightfall. They had already spent one uneasy night sleeping on the floor of the forest with only their cloaks wrapped around them. Elric hardly rested at all. The entire night he feared brigands or thieves would come upon them in the dark.

All day long, they had been fighting the forest. They couldn't find a good path. Most of the trails had been washed out in the storm. The ground was still soft from the rain and large branches, or sometimes entire fallen trees, laid across their path. A sick feeling turned in his stomach. He had never been to the cloister, and didn't know exactly how to get there. His only clue was to continue to wander north in the hope that they would find civilization.

Father had said he got the apple from a market in a large town by a fork in the river. If they found the river, they could follow it north until they found the right fork. The town would be nearby, and someone there would have to know the location of the cloister. Wynn could become a nun. She was good at memorizing things. She could remember her prayers and live with the other women somewhere that was safe.

In the meantime they needed to avoid the roads and stay out of sight. Their father would be searching for them, and if Cuthbert found out they ran away, he would make sure they ended up whipped, or put in the stocks, or worse, once they returned home.

"Is it a long way?" Wynn asked.

"Not so very far," Elric said, though he had no idea if that was the truth. "Let's hurry."

He set out with long strides, and Wynn followed along after him, humming to herself. A narrow deer path wandered along the edge of a thicket and around an enormous fallen oak. The roots branched skyward. The tree reminded Elric of a slain giant with a beard full of snakes. An unsettled feeling came over him. It was too quiet.

"Wynn?" He spun around. She wasn't there. "Wynn!" he shouted.

She emerged from behind the thick trunk of a tree some distance behind him. He watched in disbelief as she stooped and picked up a stick, inspected it, and tucked it under the strap of her sack. She had amassed a small bundle of sticks on her shoulder, and bent to pick up another.

"What are you doing?" Elric splashed in a puddle in his haste to reach her. The cold water soaked into his stocking until his toes squished in his shoe.

"I'm helping," she said with a bright smile, shoving the stick in with the others tucked under her sack.

Elric had to take a breath to hold back his frustration.

Carrying a bunch of sticks would only slow them down. "You're wasting time. Now come on, and keep up."

Once, just once, Elric wished Wynn would do what he asked her to do when he asked her to do it without wandering off and picking some flowers somewhere, or packing a chicken in her sack.

He hated to admit it, but when they reached the cloister, it would be a relief. He glanced back just to make sure Wynn was still following. Thankfully she was, only a step behind him, her eyes cast down to her feet.

The path twisted into a grove of trees with a thick carpet of fallen leaves. Elric kept to bare ground along an embankment to avoid ticks. They walked in silence for several minutes until Elric heard a rustling nearby.

"Wynn! I told you to stay close—" He stopped and turned, and Wynn almost ran into him.

He heard it again in the trees behind them.

Someone was following them.

"Quick, behind here." Elric grabbed Wynn and forced her around the blackened hull of a tree that had been burned at some point. He tucked himself against the rough bark and held his arm over her chest to keep her still.

There was a sharp crackle.

And another.

Elric's fear grew with every breath he took. He pulled his short knife from his belt. It could be Father—maybe he had tracked them all this time. Or bandits, or even a mad dog. His sister clung to his arm, but didn't say a word.

Awwwwwwk . . . cluck . . . cluck . . . cluck.

A very fat black hen with dark brown mottled spots on her wings and a bright red comb scratched at the dead leaves.

"Mildred!" Wynn nearly pushed him down the embankment as she ran to the bird. She scooped Mildred up in her arms and lovingly stroked her neck.

Elric slumped against the tree trunk, feeling shaky from leftover fear. This was the last thing he needed.

"Put her down and leave her. We can't take a chicken with us," Elric said as he started back down the path.

"Why?" Wynn asked, tucking the hen under her arm. The bird cocked her head to the side and gave him an imperious look.

"Because she will slow us down." Elric marched on. If they kept going this direction, they were sure to come to the river, but he wasn't certain if they were on the right side of it.

"Why?" Wynn insisted.

"I don't know!" Elric shouted at her.

Wynn took a step back, and placed the hen on the ground. She didn't say anything, but she could never hide how she was feeling. It always showed on her face. Her eyes were wide, and she frowned. She looked confused, but also fearful.

He let out a huff of air. "We have to find the river before nightfall and we can't afford any more delays. I'm trying to help you."

Wynn reached out and took his hand. "I'm trying to help."

Elric looked down at his feet. She was repeating again—every time something upset her it made it harder for her to think of words on her own. He couldn't afford to upset her either. That would also slow them down. "I know." He adjusted the sack looped over his shoulder. "Let's just go."

They set off down the path, and the hen followed. Elric tried to shoo her back toward home, but the bird shook her comb and stared at him as if he were a strange curiosity.

It continued on this way for some time. They moved forward, only to have Elric turn around and chase the hen several paces back in an attempt to force the stubborn bird to give up and return to where she belonged.

"Wynn, tell your hen to go home," he said as she stooped to pick up another stick.

She looked at him strangely. "She's a chicken."

"I know she's a chicken." Elric had to fight to keep from shouting the words in his frustration. Elric picked up a stone and threw it at the bird. The hen fluttered up and landed on Wynn's bundle of sticks.

"Just get out of here, you worthless bird!" he shouted at the hen.

"Leave her alone!" Wynn backed away from him, turning her shoulder so the bundle of sticks and the useless bird were as far from him as possible.

Everything with his sister became more difficult when she decided to be stubborn. "Mildred shouldn't be following us," he insisted.

"She likes me." Wynn set off down the trail without him. The chicken's upright tail pointed skyward like a jaunty flag of victory above the fluffy rump facing him. Wynn didn't bother to look back. "You are wasting time," she called, again borrowing his words.

"Fine, have it your way," Elric grumbled. The hen fluffed her black feathers and settled down on the swaying bundle of sticks. Once he got Wynn to the cloister, the hen wouldn't matter. He just hoped the nuns wouldn't immediately turn Mildred into soup.

They continued on for hours through small patches of woods and the edges of muddy spring fields. Thankfully they saw no one. The only sound was Mildred softly clucking from her perch on Wynn's stack of sticks, and Wynn singing the song of the Fairy Queen under her breath.

> *"The road begins at my feet,*
> *And leads me ever on.*
> *To the land that lies between,*
> *The first light and the dawn.*
> *I seek the favor of the queen*
> *Within that magic land.*
> *Please grant to me your silver branch,*
> *And through the gate I'll find you."*

The woods thinned and opened to an enormous field. A flock of starlings rose, taking wing like an enormous black cloud that covered the sky for a mile before them.

"That's amazing," Wynn called as she watched the birds defy the earthy bounds and stretch, flow, and ebb, filling the air. "They're dancing."

Elric watched the flock, amazed by the mass of it.

Wynn laughed, and sang the song of the Fairy Queen louder. The thick murmuration of birds seemed to respond to her. They flowed with the melody of the song, sweeping high and then low. The flock expanded outward until he could see the individual birds, then collapsed into a tight black mass, then spread once more in a different direction as the sun set behind the trees.

And still Wynn sang,

"My queen, my queen, I'll sing with joy,
And loyalty proclaim.
Smoke dances to my gift of song,
And water turns to flame.
Please grant to me your silver branch,
And through the gate I'll find you."

Elric watched the birds and was struck by the fact that they did resemble a great cloud of smoke churning through a flaming sky. But he knew it was nothing more than a fantasy. He wished he could believe otherwise.

Wynn let the notes of the song fade, and the birds settled back down onto the field.

Elric had seen large murmurations of starlings take flight before. He knew that the birds were responding to light and shifts in the wind, not a changeling girl's song. That would be impossible. And yet as he listened, he could swear the birds were saying, "This way, this way!" Elric shook his head to try to hear more clearly. The words changed to "Wynn, this way, Wynn, this way."

"Look! The river," Wynn said, pointing west.

He didn't have time to wonder about the calls of the birds anymore, so great was his surprise. The river, swollen by the recent rains flooded into the far side of the low-lying fields. The glittering surface reflected the pinks and orange of the sunset, transforming it into a river of fire flowing through the countryside.

"Come on," Elric urged.

Wynn's hen fluttered down from her shoulder as they ran through the field of chattering starlings. The birds took flight again, but only enough to let them pass, then settled back down to feast on the newly seeded barley, creating an eerily straight path through the flock.

They reached a grove of trees near the river, and Elric let his sack slide off his shoulder. The distant voices of the starlings sounded like muffled conversations. He tried to parse out their words. "She'll come. This way. Wynn, this way."

Elric dug his finger into his ear as the hen trotted into the grove and pecked at the ground. He was hearing things, that had to be it, nothing but a trick of the mind.

"We shouldn't continue in the dark," Elric said as he inspected the small clearing. There were no signs of flooding here, unlike the areas closer to the riverbanks. Lines of sticks and dead leaves marked the edge of the high water, and they were well above the floodline. Elric and Wynn should be safe for the night. They needed light, but the trees were thin here, and young. He wasn't sure if they'd find enough dry deadfall to create a strong fire. His heart raced. They'd be more vulnerable in the dark and dusk was descending quickly. They were losing what little light they had. It wouldn't be enough. "We'll need to start a—"

Wynn pulled her sack off her shoulder. It hit the ground with a clatter as the bundle of dried wood she had amassed fell at their feet.

She crossed her arms.

"—fire," Elric finished. He would never live this down.

CHAPTER SEVEN

Elric

ELRIC PROPPED HIS WET FOOT up near the flames of their fire and leaned back on a fallen log. Wynn sat on the log and rested her elbows on her knees and her chin in her hands.

She started singing softly again as the light around them dimmed. The lilting and whimsical verses always fell down to a haunting and sad note at the end. After hearing it over and over the notes wound into his head until they lodged there, and he knew he wouldn't be able to get them out.

"Enough. You've sung that song fifty times today." He poked at the fire with a long stick to knock down some of the flames. He wanted it hot, but not too bright. They didn't need to attract any attention from thieves.

"I like singing," Wynn said as she slid down the log so she could sit beside him. Mildred hopped into her lap and made a nest in her skirt. "It's pretty." Wynn sang louder, off-key as usual. Elric did not say what he was thinking: it was *not* pretty. But he didn't like to discourage her. It took her a long time to get good at things. Maybe one day she would be good at this, too. He winced as she sang a particularly loud and discordant note. (Or, maybe she wouldn't.) To his dismay, Mildred joined in, stretching her neck straight up as she let out a loud, warbling *bwaaaaawk!* and then clucked happily.

How did he get himself into this? Elric closed his eyes and sure enough, the song was stuck in his head. He could hear his mother's voice singing it as she cooked a kettle of roots and herbs over the fire. Her voice sounded clear and sure, not muddled with half the words forgotten. As he heard the tune in his head, he felt warmer, safer, not so far from home.

Bwaaaaawk! Cluck, cluck, cluck!

Wynn giggled merrily and stroked the hen.

"Ugh," Elric grumbled. "Both of you, stop it. You're ruining the song."

"You sing!" Wynn gave him a bright smile and waited. Even Mildred stared at him with an expectant look on her face.

"No." Elric kicked his other foot up and leaned back, closing his eyes.

"He's no fun," Wynn muttered. The chicken gave a sympathetic *tuk tuk tuk*.

For a long time the only sounds were the crackling of the fire, the low clucking of the hen, and the soft hush of the river behind them.

"What will you do where we are going?" Wynn asked, breaking the silence as the shadows around them deepened.

"What do you mean?" Elric tossed a broken piece of dead wood on the fire. The rain-damp bark hissed. "I'll make sure you are safe, then go tend the sheep."

"They have sheep?" Wynn's smile brightened.

Elric hesitated. Wynn thought he was going to stay with the nuns. He didn't know how to explain this to her, and considered lying, but it would be better to face this now, rather than at the cloister gate. She looked at him with adoration as she petted her hen, and suddenly

Elric felt very small. "I have to go back home to tend the flock for the villagers." He leaned his head on the log, the bark scratching his neck.

Wynn scooped Mildred up and hugged her close to her chest. "You won't stay?"

Sometimes he wished she could figure out some of these things on her own.

"I can't stay. I'm taking you to a convent. Only women are allowed inside. You will have to do your chores and remember your prayers, but the nuns will keep you safe."

Wynn stood, leaves and sticks clinging to her skirts. "I don't want to go. I will stay with you."

"You can't!" Elric pushed himself up to catch her, afraid she might get up and run back home.

Tears formed in Wynn's big blue eyes.

"Don't cry." Elric reached out and pulled Wynn into a hug, but she didn't wrap her arms around him. "It's going to be fine."

Wynn still didn't say anything.

"I'm trying to protect you." Elric pulled back so he could look her in the face. Her tears rolled over her round cheeks. "It's what Mother would have wanted."

Wynn's brow furrowed, and the tangled strands of

her long hair hung around her face from where they escaped the braid their mother had woven before she died. Wynn couldn't even keep her hair neat on her own. She pushed the mess out of her eyes wiping her tears as she did. "Mother always kept me near."

She had to. That was the problem, she had to. Mother had hidden herself and Wynn away in the woods so well that most in the village assumed she had died during Wynn's birth, and the baby soon after. If anyone saw them, if anyone knew, Mother could have been accused of witchcraft for keeping a changeling child alive so long. Elric felt a heaviness pulling on his heart, and he didn't know how to fix it. Wynn turned away and walked to the edge of the shadows, and flopped down in a tangle of roots.

Elric sat on the log with a sigh. If there were any other way, he would do it. If there were some way he could care for her, he would do it. But he was just a boy, and bound to obey both his father and their lord. He couldn't disappear into the woods and hide her there. They would starve before winter, and the village needed someone to care for the animals. Eventually he would have to take over his father's land and continue to toil under his bond to their lord. Living away from the protection of the armies was too risky. They could be attacked by robbers, or raiding armies from other lands.

Maybe if he were grown, they could find a way to live as hermits in the woods, but he wasn't a man yet. He couldn't keep her with him.

That didn't mean he wouldn't miss her.

Under his breath he began to sing a verse of the fairy song. It's what Mother would have done for her. Wynn hunched her shoulders as she huddled closer to the tree and pulled her cloak more tightly around her neck.

> *"My queen, my queen, I seek the path,*
> *To the land Between.*
> *With your power great and fair,*
> *Show me what's unseen.*
> *Please grant to me your silver branch,*
> *And through the gate I'll find you."*

He sang louder as he walked toward her, adding a little skip and a hop, a part of a dance she had made up when they were little.

She still refused to look at him.

He sat down next to her and placed his arm over her shoulders. "What's the next verse? I have forgotten it. Something about the moon and stars?"

Wynn didn't respond.

"I don't want to leave you, either," he confessed in a soft voice. "I promise I will come to visit when I can," he said, holding her close to his side.

She leaned her head against him. "I'll wait for you."

Elric continued to sing through his tight throat. In two more verses, she had fallen fast asleep. Elric watched over her through the deep part of night.

As dawn broke, Elric heard an ox bellow in the distance and the rumbling of a cart. A curl of smoke rose from their small fire. He shook Wynn awake.

"Come on. I think there's a road nearby." He pushed himself up out of the tangle of tree roots, his limbs aching and tingling. His eyes burned with exhaustion. If they were lucky, they would find the cloister before nightfall.

Wynn stretched and pushed her hair away from her face. "I'm hungry."

Elric picked up her sack and opened it. Then he remembered it was full of ripped-up weeds and an old pot. He let it fall to the ground. It was a waste of energy lifting it at all. "Look in my sack. There's a bit of bread, but don't eat it all."

Elric took his time smothering the fire before

turning back to Wynn. She was holding the crust of the bread down as the hen pecked furiously at it.

"Wynn!" He ran toward her, shooing the chicken away.

"She is hungry too." Wynn stood and brushed the crumbs off her skirt.

"We can't waste food," Elric insisted, snatching the crust away from her and shoving it back in his bag. He hefted it over his shoulder.

"I don't like that part." Wynn picked up her own sack and pulled the strings tight before shouldering her bag full of weeds.

"Come on," he said as he followed the river upstream. "And try not to be a bother."

Wynn dropped her gaze to her feet and walked sullenly behind him, her hen clucking alongside her.

They walked in silence most of the morning along the banks of the river until finally they found the road. A steady stream of people followed it toward a rise of hills in the distance. He could see the tops of buildings, a grand town, much larger than their poor village.

"Stay quiet," Elric warned as he approached a bent old man leading a small herd of goats. "Ho there," he called.

The goatherd looked back and gave Elric a toothless smile. "On your way to market?" he asked.

"Of course." Elric said a quick prayer of thanks. With market going on, there would be a lot of strange people in the town. He and Wynn could blend in. "Father sent us to buy a pig."

"Buy a pig?" Wynn asked. Elric turned and glared at her, but she just looked at him, confused.

"What was that?" the old man asked, turning to Wynn. "Hello there."

"Hello!" she greeted, her face transforming as she gave him a wide smile. "I like your goats."

"I like your chicken," he said.

"It's a gift for the cloister. Do you know where it is?" Elric asked.

"You said—"

Elric nudged his sister hard with his elbow. "Not now."

"Hmm, yes. Take the north road out of town," the goatherd said. "Follow it past the woods and through the orchards. You will find the cloister there."

"Thank you!" Elric pulled Wynn along until they could walk side by side on the road without anyone else hearing.

"Why did you do that?" Wynn asked, rubbing her arm where he had jabbed her.

"Just don't speak to anyone. Please."

"I know," Wynn replied in a frustrated voice as she rubbed her arm.

Crowds of people had gathered along the road, all flowing closer to the gates. Music from a man playing a reed pipe drifted over the noise of the crowd. Wynn bumped into a woman because she had turned to watch a juggler throwing small colorful sacks high in the air as he walked.

"Ooh," Wynn said, pointing to the juggler. "That's amazing."

The energy of market day got under his skin, and Elric smiled at the look on Wynn's face. She had never seen anything like this in her lonely little hut in the woods. To be honest, he'd never seen anything like it either, and the excitement was contagious.

"I can do that; watch," he said, smiling at her. He picked up three small rocks from the road and tossed them gently in the air, but only managed to catch one as it came back down. One of them hit him on the top of his head. He winced and rubbed the spot where it hit. Wynn laughed so hard she started hiccupping. "Hey, it's trickier than it looks!"

She snorted. "Do it again." She bent and picked up the stones.

"I don't think I make a very good jester," Elric said to her, and she giggled through a hiccup.

The thatched roofs of buildings peeked over the top of the wooden wall that surrounded the town, as the chatter of people and animals drifted through the air. It wasn't the only thing that drifted through the air. The smell of filth and putrid meat hung like a cloud around them, and grew worse as they arrived near the gates.

Elric covered his nose with his sleeve as he trudged forward, but Wynn stopped, looking up over a deep moat of blood from the butchers and animal carcasses rotting in a pit outside the gates. A cloud of flies swarmed over the pit, buzzing near their ears. One landed on Elric's neck and gave him a stinging bite. Elric slapped it away, but a smear of blood streaked over his palm. They had to get out of there. He tugged on Wynn's sleeve, but she didn't move. Instead, she pointed.

Three tiny iron cages hung over the pit. In the central cage, the deep, empty sockets of a man's skull stared at them, his teeth bared in a terrible grin. Thankfully the other two were unoccupied, except for bits of rotten cloth clinging to the bottom bars that proved they had not always been empty.

"What did he do?" Wynn asked, then coughed, and shook her head as another horsefly buzzed between them.

"I don't know," Elric said. "Just stay close to me."

Wynn stroked her hen and drew herself near her brother's side. "Stay close," she repeated as she slipped her sack off her shoulder and tucked Mildred inside.

Inside the town, the oppressive smell of death eased, replaced by fires and the scent of livestock and leather. Buildings loomed over them, their second floors hanging above the narrow streets. Elric didn't like the way they leaned, as if they were about to topple over. At the center of the town, market stalls had been hastily tied together with wooden posts and bits of canvas to shade the wares. The market cross stood high on a stone pillar, where the money-counters gathered holding their scales aloft.

The sights and sounds of the market were overwhelming, and Elric felt buffeted on every side by people. He pushed through the crowd. They had to make it to the cloister before nightfall. Once they found the north gate, then it would be easy to find the right road and the crowds would thin. Colorful flags of woven cloth fluttered on long ropes strung between the windows of the tilting buildings. According to the direction of the shadows, they would have to keep moving forward, then turn left.

In an alcove, a butcher carved mutton off the carcass of a young sheep. Elric paused to watch, keenly aware that they had only bits of stale bread. His mouth watered at the idea of roast mutton. Soon. He would be home soon. "Come on. Let's hurry."

He reached back, offering his hand. No one took it. Elric turned around. Wynn was no longer by his side.

His stomach turned to stone and dropped through to his shoes as he searched the crowd for her. Hundreds of people crisscrossed the open market, stopping at stalls. They wove paths in and out of the brief gaps that opened in the crowd, before those small pockets of space filled with more people. A loud shout and a cheer went up from a cluster of people with their backs to him.

Elric pressed into the wall of bodies and caught a glimpse of a dwarf man wearing a jester's cap, and riding on the back of a very fat goat, but didn't pay any heed. Instead he inspected the mass of people for Wynn's face, but there was no sign of her.

His heart picked up. He had to find her.

A cloud passed over the sun, dimming the bright marketplace. He heard a young man laugh to his left. It was the kind of laugh that carried a cruel edge. It stopped Elric in his tracks. He had heard that sort of laugh before. "You want to buy a pig? I can sell you a pig."

Elric followed the sound of the boy's voice to a short stone wall surrounding a deep pig wallow. A group of four older boys had gathered around Wynn and smiled at her with dark grins and cruel, glinting eyes.

The oldest of the lot put his hand over Wynn's shoulder. "All you have to do is climb into the pen and pick the one you want."

No.

He pushed past the villagers crossing in front of him until he reached Wynn's side. Her wide smile shone in her eyes as she looked adoringly at the older boy.

"Get away from her!" Elric shouted, throwing the boy's arm off his sister's shoulder. The boy slid his filthy palm over Wynn's long braid and gave it a tug.

Wynn beamed at him as if nothing was wrong. "He is going to sell us a pig."

"No, he's not." Elric took Wynn by the arm and

pushed her behind him. He had to look up at the leader of the boys, whose chin was already growing a scraggly beard.

"Well, look at that. This little boy is speaking against my good nature." He laughed again, and Elric's blood ran cold. "Am I not a man of my word?"

His friends laughed in chorus, a malicious sound he knew too well. It was the kind he heard when people threw things at someone in the stocks. Elric took a step back, but the older boys pushed closer.

He glanced around, looking for anyone that could help them. No one was watching. Everyone else was taken by the sights and sounds of the market and paid no heed to a bunch of kids standing near a wallow.

Elric caught the eye of the dwarf, standing in his fool's cap as he scratched the back of his goat's neck. He had been watching what was happening, and Elric could see him frowning.

"Let's go," Elric said, taking his sister's hand.

"But we haven't completed our sale." The tallest boy lunged for Wynn. "She needs to choose her pig. In the pen, half-wit."

Suddenly the jester ran toward them, hollering and screaming incoherent nonsense. The group of boys stumbled backward in shock, parting the way a flock of sheep does for a well-trained dog. The man threw himself face-first into the slop of mud near a large pigpen and rolled around, howling as his goat ran forward and butted him on his behind.

The boys fell into peals of laughter at the jester's antics, holding their sides as they doubled over in their mirth.

"Run," Elric whispered, shoving Wynn hard in the back. They dodged through the crowd, weaving as fast as they could through the busy market. Wynn clung to her sack, and Elric gripped her wrist so tightly, he knew his nails were digging into her flesh, but she didn't protest. Elric found the north gate and slipped through it, pushing against the tides of people coming to the town for market.

Once they were safely outside of the crowds, Elric let Wynn go. She breathed heavily as she dropped her sack to the ground. Mildred poked her head out the top, then struggled out of the sack. The ruffled hen shook her feathers and trotted away into the shade of the nearby trees.

"Why did we run?" Wynn asked, her strange-sounding words even more muddled by her heavy breaths.

Elric let his head fall as he struggled to ease the cramp in his side. "You wouldn't understand."

Wynn opened her mouth as if she wanted to say something, but then closed it. She blinked and looked away from him. "They were nice."

"No, they weren't. They were trying to trick you." Elric straightened and adjusted his sack on his shoulder.

"Why?" Wynn came in close to his side.

"Because they think it's funny." He looped his arm over her shoulder and together they walked up the road.

"I don't understand," Wynn said.

Elric took a deep breath and waited for his panic to ease. He shook his head. "I don't either."

The cloister wasn't far now. The sooner they got there, the better.

CHAPTER EIGHT

Elric

THE LONG ROAD WANDERED INTO a thick grove of trees that turned to a neat orchard bursting with apple blooms. Elric thought that the trees smelled like heaven compared to the town they just left behind. Come fall, the trees would be teeming with fruit. Wynn would have apples to eat whenever she wanted. Elric smiled as he remembered the way she constantly got into the honey when they were little—she always did have a sweet tooth. Plus, chewing apples would help strengthen her mouth so she could speak better. Between the trees, the road narrowed until it was little more than a cart path that wound through the orchard.

Finally the path ended at a formidable stone building, two stories high with a peaked roof and tiny dark windows every ten feet. Elric couldn't see a chapel, only an enormous wooden door like a strange frowning mouth on the face of the stone building. He didn't know what he was expecting when he thought of the convent, but this building intimidated him. It seemed so cold. For the first time he wondered, what would happen if the nuns didn't take Wynn in? What would they do?

The nuns had to show her mercy. Wynn would be fine. He rubbed the wooden spoon tucked in his belt.

"This must be it," Elric said as he forced his voice to sound unnaturally pleasant.

Wynn slowed and crossed her arms. "The walls are very big."

Wynn was right. Elric couldn't see anything beyond them, not even a spire or cross. It felt like the world ended here. "The walls will protect you. Come on."

Elric pounded on the rough wood, then turned to Wynn. "Don't speak," he said hastily. "Just in case."

A small window in the door opened. A young woman with a sweet expression framed by her pale gray wimple peered at them through the gap. "Oh, I beg your pardon. I thought you were our sisters come back from market. Can I help you?"

"My sister wishes to join you," Elric said, his throat tight. This was for the best.

The young nun gave Wynn a soft smile, and Wynn tucked herself behind Elric in response. "I'll alert the abbess." The window shut, leaving them alone in the shadow of the high walls.

"I want to go away," Wynn said. Elric turned around to face her. He placed his hands on her shoulders and looked her in the eye. Their downward tilt seemed more pronounced with the deep sadness he saw there. He felt it in his chest.

"They have apples." Elric gave her shoulders a squeeze. "And on the inside of the walls, I'm sure there is a lovely garden and many kind women like the one at the door."

Wynn stepped forward and pressed her head against Elric's shoulder as she hugged him so tightly, he had trouble breathing. "I miss you."

His eyes stung. He thought about all the times he left to mind the flock. She would wave until he feared her arm would fall off, and when he returned, she would run to him with the biggest smile and knock him over in her attempt to hug him. There would be no return this time. No more of her wild laughter at the silliest things. No more joy in his family. No more family at all, really.

"I'll miss you too, little sister."

The heavy door creaked as it opened, revealing a tall woman with a narrow face and pointy chin. Her mouth was little more than a thin line in her face, and she kept it tightly pinched in a scowl. The undyed wool of her habit was much finer than the other woman's. The cloth fell over her like a blanket of snow as she kept her hands hidden in the deep folds of her massive sleeves, but her clothing did little to soften her appearance.

She looked down her long nose at Wynn and the wrinkles of her forehead deepened. "You may come for alms on Sunday."

There was no mercy in her voice, and her words sounded final. Just like that, she'd decided Wynn couldn't live there. The only mercy she would show a soul in need was to tell her to show up on Sunday so she could fight for whatever food and coins they threw out into the crowd of beggars. "We're not looking for charity," Elric said, his voice cracking. "Our parents are gone, and I can't care for my sister alone. She's a hard worker and would obey you at all times. She can weed the garden or clean the floors." The young nun stepped up behind the abbess, staying in the shadows, her kind eyes wide with sympathy.

"Is this true?" the abbess said to Wynn, who looked up at the holy woman but didn't say anything. She just stared. "Well, do you speak?" The voice of the abbess became harsh.

Wynn looked away, and then to her worn shoes. Her face scrunched up, as if finding any words at all in her mind physically pained her. "Elric said no talking."

Elric's hope sank as her words came out as garbled as ever. Even he had trouble understanding them.

The abbess turned her hard gaze on Elric and he felt as if he were shrinking down to the size of a dormouse. "You bring an unnatural child born out of God's grace to the house of the Lord, and expect to find welcome here? She is a changeling."

She wasn't unnatural. She just didn't talk well. Why was that so wrong? He knew lots of people who weren't the quickest thinkers. They weren't treated this way. Wynn never did anything wrong. His face flushed with the heat of his anger even as desperation became a fire in his stomach. "She's good!" Elric protested. "She doesn't speak well, but she can do chores. She needs help."

"She could be a lay-sister and feed the geese. I could

teach her prayers," the young nun said from behind the abbess's shoulder.

The older woman turned and stared at the younger one. Not a single thing about her expression changed, but the young nun immediately bowed her head in submission and folded her hands.

"I will not expose this abbey to an unfit soul." The abbess turned her hard glare back to Wynn, as if she could crush her with the power of her words. "We have taken a vow of poverty. What resources we have must be devoted to God and the *good* women who come here from noble families to pursue their devotion and study. We must not waste." She glanced back at the young nun behind her. "Return to your cell and pray for God's mercy."

And with that she turned and walked back into the high stone walls, shutting the door behind her.

Elric felt suddenly sick. He held his stomach as he turned away from the door and stumbled on the dark road. Wynn came quickly to his side and held his arm to steady him.

"I'm sorry," she said. "I spoke and you said not to."

"It's not your fault," Elric said, but he had to force the words out. Where were they supposed to go now? They couldn't return home. Father would be waiting.

They had no place else they could go. Little food, no shelter. Rainstorms and snow would prove dangerous. They'd end up beggars holding out their hands for alms from the church that had thrown them out in the deadly cold.

"Does God not like me?" Wynn asked, glancing back at the convent.

"He is supposed to love everyone." Elric adjusted the sack on his shoulder. God was not supposed to be vengeful and cruel.

"Like a father," Wynn said as she stooped to pick up Mildred.

Elric let out a heavy breath. "Yes, like Father."

Wynn looked as if a little piece of her soul had been crushed.

Elric heard the scraping of a latch, then the slow creak of a hinge opening behind them. Now what?

"Come here," the soft voice of the young nun called through the open window. She waved to them, beckoning them closer. "Quickly."

Wynn trotted up to the door. The young nun pushed a tied cloth through the hole. "Take these. They're my rations for tonight. They're not much, but they will help you on your way."

Wynn gathered the small sack from the nun's hands.

"Thank you," Wynn said as the young woman's hand retreated.

"Go, with God's blessing." She gave them one last smile before she shut the window, leaving them alone on the darkening road.

"Where do we go?" Wynn asked. She hugged Mildred tight.

Elric reached out and stroked Mildred's feathers. The hen clucked sleepily. "I don't know," he said. "But we can't stay here."

They would have to go back to the town they'd just fled from. In the town he could attempt to use his skills to support them. If they were lucky, he could find work as a shepherd or with a butcher. But he had no one to speak for his character. People were wary of strangers, and his circumstances were suspicious. Good people didn't leave the land they were bound to. It would disrupt everything if serfs in the countryside refused to work the land they were given.

Maybe the wilderness was their best chance. They would have to live like nomads, but that brought its own challenges, like finding food. He wasn't a good hunter and didn't have a bow. He could make a sling, but a sling would hardly feed them. And he had no saw or ax, no way to make shelter.

Perhaps they should return home. He could apologize to Father, but then he would have to watch Wynn be led off like a lamb to the slaughter, to a world where he knew she would suffer.

She leaned against him, nudging him out of his dark thoughts. "Don't be sad," she said. "We're together."

"Always." He took her hand and led them both down the road with Mildred following close behind.

They arrived back at the town just before the sun set. What had been a full and bustling town center now looked deserted, with merchants tearing down their rickety stalls for the night. The buildings cast the streets in shadow as Elric and Wynn had to dodge pots of foul water being thrown from the high windows.

The smell of filth rose from the ground as night settled over them.

"We need to find a place to hide, or we'll end up in the stocks," Elric warned. He led them down a narrow street and the sound of laughter poured from of a nearby inn. Elric stopped short and held his arm protectively across Wynn as a group of young men stumbled out of the open door.

They staggered before drawing themselves up, their

cruel laughter too familiar, then turned their bloodshot gazes to Wynn.

"Well, well! It's Pig Girl." The tall one pointed at Wynn. "The one with the pretty hair. Hate to see it get dirty." His words slurred together as he drew his hand through the mud at his feet, then flung it up at Wynn's face.

She cried out when the thick glop hit her above the ear and fell down on her long braid. The group burst into howls of laughter.

"Leave her alone!" Elric shouted, balling his fists. He could feel the heat in his face as his heart thundered to life.

"She's nothing but a half-wit. It's not like it matters," a second boy cackled. "Oh, look, she's crying."

Elric reached out to Wynn, tears streaming down her face as she clutched Mildred to her chest.

"I can make her cry worse," a short and fat boy said. "Hand me that chicken. I'll break its neck."

"Touch her and you'll pay," Elric growled at them.

"You'll make us pay?" the leader asked, pushing up his sleeves. "This might be worth the price, boys."

"Run, Wynn!" Elric shouted. "Run!"

CHAPTER NINE
Wynn

WYNN RAN DOWN THE ROAD. She held Mildred tight. She wouldn't let that boy hurt her hen. Mildred was special. Her claws caught Wynn's forearm and scratched. It stung, but Wynn held fast. She wouldn't let go of her Mildred.

She heard a shout. She turned to see Elric bent over, holding his stomach. Another boy hit him across the face and he fell.

"Elric!" Wynn screamed. She wanted to go back and help him, but he told her to run. Elric was clever, and she had to listen to him. But he was hurt.

A rock hit her head. She flinched as pain throbbed through her scalp. She saw the boy who wanted to kill Mildred. He was catching up to her, picking up another rock.

She had to run.

She turned and fled. Elric was hurt. She was hurt too. Mildred couldn't die.

Run.

Her feet splashed through the mud as she came near the gate. Another rock flew past and skipped over the road in front of her.

Keep running.

She passed through the gate. The skull in the cage still smiled at her. She didn't want to breathe because it stank here, but she was running too hard to stop.

She panted as she held tight to Mildred. Her sack slipped from her shoulder and caught in the crook of her elbow. It slapped against her side with each step.

The bad ones were still behind her. She had to hide, like the fox Mother had chased from the gardens. It liked to disappear in bushes.

The woods had bushes.

She turned off the road and slid down a hill, her

skirts tangling around her feet as the wet leaves and mud coated her legs. There were bushes up ahead.

Wynn threw Mildred. The hen flapped her short wings, then landed heavily on the ground and sprinted into the shrubs. Mildred was very black and it was dark. No one would find her now.

Wynn looked back at the road, just in time to see the bad person who threw rocks at her fall into the ditch. He shouted something she didn't understand, then rubbed the mud off his face.

Keep running.

Wynn pushed through the bushes, then ran through the trees. Only the moonlight showed her way, and the shadows under the forest roof were dark.

Her toes caught on a tree root and she fell hard. Hot tears trailed over her face as she stayed down in the fallen leaves.

Mildred was gone. Elric was gone. Her whole body shook. She clamped her teeth together to keep them from chattering and tried to look around, but she couldn't see anything except bushes and leaves. Her cloak draped over her like a blanket, and she curled her body up to hide beneath it.

She felt something gently nudge her elbow.

Wynn turned her head and gasped.

Lying beneath a bush right beside her was a young doe. She stretched her neck forward and sniffed Wynn's cloak. "Hello," Wynn whispered, but the doe didn't run away. It blinked at her, then nudged her again. The doe lowered her head, tucking her face into her side. That's when Wynn understood. She needed to hide. Wynn lay her head down too, pulling her hood over her hair, and held still like the deer.

She heard the bad man stumble and curse in the woods, but the doe didn't move, so she didn't either. The doe would know when to run. Wynn would run then too. The bad man passed in front of her. She could see his muddy shoes. They smelled rotten.

He moved slowly, searching, his feet crunching in the leaves. He passed right by Wynn, and didn't see her, or the doe.

"Half-wit isn't worth it," he grumbled as he staggered away.

Once Wynn couldn't hear him anymore, she lifted her head. The doe did the same. Slowly the doe stood. Wynn pushed herself to her feet; the mud they had thrown at her was itchy on her skin, and her head still hurt from the rock. She wondered where Mildred was and hoped she was safe. Foxes lived in the woods, after all.

Wynn swung her sack on her shoulder and began walking toward the village. She needed Elric.

Turning around to remember which way she had run, she noticed the doe still standing, watching her. In the moonlight, the forest looked gray and the leaves silvery all around them. A soft wind made the trees whisper. In the quiet, danger felt far away.

Wynn watched the creature. The doe took three steps away, then faced Wynn again, her large ears turning slowly back and forth as she waited for something.

Did she want Wynn to follow?

Wynn took a hesitant step toward the deer.

The deer took another three steps deeper into the woods and looked back, waiting.

Wynn followed. This was very strange. Deer never stayed close to her before. This one was different, but she lived in the woods and would know where to go. Once the doe seemed sure Wynn was close behind, she walked steadily forward without turning back. She would only twist an ear every few steps to make sure Wynn was still following her.

They passed through a dark place in the woods, but

there was a bright spot ahead. The path opened into a clearing. The trunks of the trees and the shadows between them formed arches, like the doors of churches. The mostly round moon hung at the center of the open gap in the trees. Moonlight shimmered on soft, dewy mosses clinging to the springy forest floor within a perfect circle of rocks.

A fairy ring. It was just like the one she used to play in with Elric.

A clear running stream flowed along the edge of the circle to the left, before wandering back into the dark woods. The doe stopped and took a drink, then looked back at Wynn. She blinked once and bowed her graceful neck. Suddenly she bounded through the woods, disappearing into the thicket the way a deer should.

Wynn stood under the bright light of the moon in the circle of stones. This was a safe place. She had to find her brother and bring him here.

Slowly she made her way back, looking for her footprints in the soft earth to guide her, while leaving a trail of sticks to mark the path from where she'd been.

Finally she found the road and hurried toward the town.

She came near the gate, where the horrible cages

were, but the gates were shut.

Her heart raced. "Elric?" she called. The wooden pikes that made up the wall seemed so big.

She heard a groan.

She looked down the embankment beneath the horrible cages. In the filthy ditch, a lump moved.

"Elric!"

Wynn scuttled down the embankment and grabbed him by the arm, and he cried out in pain. Oh! He was hurt. His face was covered in blood. The things in his sack had been scattered near the filthy water.

"Wynn?" His voice was weak.

"Here I am," Wynn said. She lifted him up carefully, and he managed to stagger to his knees. She pulled him up the steep bank and laid him in the road.

She slid back down the bank to gather what things she could see. She gathered them out of the foul water and shoved them back in his sack, then looped it over her shoulder until it pressed against her satchel.

Elric managed to pull himself to his feet. He was bleeding badly. Wynn felt her tears coming. They had to leave this place. It wasn't nice. She lifted her brother's arm, placed it over her neck, and held him tight around his waist. He winced, and his head hung low, but he walked with her.

It was a good thing she was strong.

They stumbled down the bank and into the forest, but she found her first twig. Wynn kept herself bent, pretending Elric's arm across her shoulders was nothing more than a big bundle of sticks. She could carry sticks a long way. She would carry him, too. She walked in the direction the twig trail was pointing.

"Wynn?" Elric moaned. He coughed, and held his stomach. His eyes puffed up until he could not open them. She would have to see for him.

"I know the way," she said, adjusting the weight of him against her side. Her back hurt, but that didn't matter. It would stop hurting when they reached the fairy ring, so she could bear it now.

She found another twig, but Elric stumbled and she had to lift him up. The forest seemed darker here, and she wished she had the doe to follow. It was hard to see the sticks in the dark. She looked ahead, but couldn't find one.

Now she was afraid.

"I can't—" Elric tried to pull away from her, but she held on.

There! There was the stick. She led him to it, and then another. A hill rose before them. She had to use her hand to push along the ground as he leaned more of his weight on her against the steep slope.

Finally, the clearing opened up before them.

"We're here," she said, her throat dry and tight. "It is safe. I can take care of you." In the moonlight, she could see how dirty he was. Dirt wasn't good for cuts. Mother used hot water to clean. That is what she would do too.

She needed a fire.

She eased Elric down on the soft moss-covered ground near the center of the ring. "Don't worry," she said.

Pulling both sacks off her shoulder, she searched through his, but it was muddy, and it smelled bad. In the bottom, she found Elric's flint wrapped tightly with his steel. The tinder was soggy.

Wynn gathered as many sticks as she could and cleared a place in the center of the ring. She set stones around it, and one in the middle she could put her pot on. On the stones she arranged the little sticks, then pulled the bark off of twigs and pulled some dried grass. It was difficult with her fat thumbs, but she managed.

Her hands fumbled with the flint. She struck it, but nothing happened. Her tears rolled over her cheeks. They splashed on the stone. She wasn't good at starting fires.

Elric moaned again. He was still hurting. He needed her. If his cuts stayed dirty, he could die.

She tried again.

There was no spark.

With her voice wobbling, she began to sing. She was afraid, and the song made her feel safer.

> *"My queen, my queen, I seek the path,*
> *To the land Between.*
> *With your power great and fair,*
> *Show me what's unseen.*
> *Please grant to me your silver branch,*
> *And through the gate I'll find you."*

Wynn tried one more time, and this time the stone sparked. The spark caught on the dried grass and grew into a tiny but beautiful flame.

Wynn squeaked as she jumped up clapping her hands. The little flame flickered, and she quickly fell to her knees to blow on it.

The fire grew.

"I did it," she said, turning to Elric. His eyes were closed and he didn't answer her. He was very sick, but she would care for him. She wouldn't let the fire go out this time.

Wynn took her little pot to gather some water, singing the whole way.

CHAPTER TEN

Elric

ELRIC DRIFTED THROUGH A HAZE of darkness and agony. He couldn't move. Even if he tried to, his body wouldn't obey his thoughts. Pain flowed through him like water, and he didn't want to open his eyes because they stung so badly. He could taste blood and bile in his mouth. Something hot pressed against his temple. He wanted to struggle away from it, but struggle was beyond him.

In the distance he could hear voices singing. A woman's voice rose above them, but he couldn't understand the words. The tune seemed familiar, though. He should know it.

It hurt too much to think.

Still, the song was beautiful, and as he listened to it, his dreams drifted to a place of dancing lights and mysterious shadows playing near a forest dark and deep. The colors seemed brighter there, but he didn't trust such visions.

The song continued and in the mists of the strange grove, a woman appeared. Her skin was as dark as the rich harvest earth, and white hair floated around her like a soft cloud in a clear winter sky. She wore a dress made of ice woven with the new blossoms of the first warm days of spring. Her eyes blazed as green as the fair golden days of summer, then turned gold like ripe fields of wheat. They glowed in the dim light as she watched him from her place atop a throne carved from stone and the roots of a living tree.

She stood from her throne and walked closer to him, her expression mildly curious as the singing voices grew hushed. He could hear another voice now—one he knew too well, singing her same song over and over again. It was Wynn's voice, as off-key as it ever was, and his breath seemed to come easier as he heard it. She was safe, but where was she? He couldn't see her.

The regal woman knelt beside him and spoke. "You have grown since I last saw you," she murmured, a sad smile touching her lips. Confusion swept through him. He had never seen such a woman in his life. But then a vague memory of snowflakes muddled his vision. He could picture clearly a tall woman dressed in ice, holding a newborn baby. It lasted only a moment, and the vision was lost. The queenly woman bent over him and placed a motherly kiss on Elric's forehead.

His eyes flew open, shattering the illusion, but he still could not see. A damp cloth lay over his eyes. The clean scent of strong herbs overwhelmed him, clearing the stench of the ditch he had been laying in from his nose and mouth.

He ripped the cloth away and pried his eyes open as much as he could, but found himself squinting into soft morning light as he lifted his head. Birds chirped in the branches overhead to greet the new dawn that had not quite broken. The cool chill of night still lingered in the air.

Mildred roosted on his chest, clucking softly in contentment. The fluffy feathers beneath her tail tickled the tip of his nose.

"Gah, Mildred! Get off!" He shoved the bird from his chest and pain lanced through half his body. Lifting his hand to his head, his palm came away sticky. What was all over his face? Was it blood? He stared at his open hand, squinting through his swollen eyes. No dark smudge stained his palm, and he could faintly smell something sweet, even through his busted nose. Was it . . . honey?

"Elric?" Wynn hunched over a small but bright fire, stirring her little pot. She noticed him moving and hurried to his side.

He struggled to sit. His ribs hurt. He held his side and realized he wasn't wearing his tunic. When he looked down, his chest and stomach were covered in dark bruises.

Wynn brought him a curled piece of bark. She'd cleverly tucked a broad leaf into it to make it hold a swallow of clean water without leaking. He took it gratefully, washing the blood from his mouth. Gently he ran his tongue over his teeth to see if they were all still there.

"You're awake!" Wynn beamed at him, tucking her legs under her as she sat on the soft moss beside him. Her skirt had been cut short, and she wore the extra pair of leggings from his bag. She'd gone and ripped up her dress. Elric tried to focus, but whatever he was thinking about flew out of his mind.

Where were they, and how did they get to this place? The last thing he remembered clearly was returning to the town after they had been turned away from the cloister. He blinked as he looked around. Spongy moss covered most of the ground, and they were surrounded by the bare branches of trees. The spring buds on the tips of the branches gave the trees a yellowish-green tint with his blurred vision. Around the edges of the clearing, he could see mossy caps on dull gray stones.

She helped him sit up straighter, then she ran to the edge of the clearing and picked up a length of cloth that had been drying on a branch of a large oak. It was a piece of her skirt cut into a long strip.

She placed the end on his bruised stomach and wrapped the rest around his body until she had his ribs bound tight, but she couldn't tie the cloth at the end. He did it for her.

"Now all the dark marks are gone," she said. He realized his arm had been wrapped loosely as well. "All better."

He touched his forehead, still sticky with honey. His hair was damp and clean. On other branches, the clothes and supplies he had packed, even the sack, hung drying in the sheltering trees. Whatever she was boiling in the small pot smelled like Mother's garden. "What happened? Are you hurt?" he asked, though he winced and gasped on the last word. It even hurt to breathe.

"I'm taking care of you." She walked over to her sack and pulled out a handful of the weeds she had stuffed inside, then dropped them in the bubbling water.

"You cleaned all this?" All the spare clothes he had managed to stuff into his sack fluttered in a slight breeze. The cuts on his knuckles shone under the honey she had spread over them, but the wounds were scrubbed beneath the sticky golden substance.

"It was all dirty."

The only thing dirty in the glen now was her. Dried mud still caked in her long and matted braid. He shuddered with a sudden chill. Wynn brought him his clean tunic and helped him lift his arm so he could struggle into it. By the time he was dressed, he was out of breath and shaking from the pain.

Now that he was awake, he was starting to remember what happened.

"All we wanted was some fun."

"Why are you protecting a stupid half-wit?"

"If she's not going in the pigpen, you can go in for her."

"You've slaughtered him. Better throw him in with the other carcasses."

There was laughter, so much laughter. He had never been beaten so badly. And it was because of her. If she had just stayed near him. If she had just not talked to anyone. If she were just invisible.

"Are you hungry?" Wynn offered him a piece of the bread that the young nun had given her. He took it, but he didn't eat. His jaw hurt too much.

Not even the convent would take her in. It was the only place that would have been safe for her as a girl, but there was simply too much wrong with her, too much the world could easily see as a weakness.

Elric tried to stand, but the pain took the wind out of him. He had intended to hurry home after reaching the convent. He'd have arrived home this morning, and few would have missed him. Now, going back without punishment seemed impossible. He had abandoned his flock and run off.

Cuthbert wouldn't let that go unpunished, and another beating could kill him.

Wynn was a mess, and everywhere they went, people would stare at her and her ripped-up dress. There was no way to avoid unwanted attention now. It would only lead to more disasters like this one. He tied the strip of the skirt she had used to bandage his arm tighter and the limb throbbed. The sticky honey was getting all over everything.

"Why is there honey all over my hands?" he demanded, once again struggling to stand and finding his feet. His head spun, but he closed his eyes against the dizzy sensation until he felt steady.

"Mother puts honey on cuts," she said simply, bringing two more strips of cloth. She tried to wrap one around his hand, but ended up twisting it wrong.

"Give me that," he said, pulling his hand away and tying it himself. "What good could honey do?" he grumbled, mostly to himself. "All it does is make things sticky."

"I don't know," Wynn answered.

"You don't know anything," he muttered. Like the fact she shouldn't speak to strangers.

Wynn blinked at him, her downward-slanted eyes wide with confusion. "I know things."

Elric let out an exasperated huff. "That's not what I meant. We're in trouble. We can't go back home, or we'll be punished. We can't stay at the convent, and we can't stay here." He tried to take a step but a sharp pain stabbed through his ankle and he almost fell back down again. "Father will never forgive this, Cuthbert will demand we're punished, and you've ruined your dress."

"I made bandages."

"That's not the point, Wynn!" he shouted. It made his head and jaw ache. He placed his head in his palms, but touched the honey again. If she stood out before, she'd only stand out more now that her kirtle dress looked like a boy's tunic.

If only she *were* a boy. People never questioned whether a boy wandering out in the woods or traveling through market was supposed to be there. Even when he spent weeks alone in the woods, or traveling with the flock, no one ever looked at him and saw an easy victim. If Wynn looked like a boy, Elric could pretend she was his younger brother and no one would think twice about it. They'd assume there was nothing wrong as long as Wynn didn't speak. Brothers were free to travel alone without hassle. A girl in a dress as short as a tunic, wearing men's leggings, would attract attention that they didn't need. Not after what just happened. But Wynn could never pass for a boy.

Unless . . .

His knife gleamed next to the fire.

There was one way to make her blend in, and he didn't have a choice.

He limped over to the knife and picked it up.

CHAPTER ELEVEN
Wynn

WYNN WAS SO HAPPY. ELRIC was standing, which meant he would be better soon. Maybe now that he was up, he could help her brush and braid her hair the way Mother always had. It was difficult for her to do it because her hands never cooperated when she tried, and she couldn't move them the right way once they were behind her head and she couldn't see them.

She had worked hard all night. She cleaned most of their things, but didn't have time to clean her own things. Elric was more important. She used all her honey on his cuts, which made her sad because she liked honey, and she had been sneaking little bits of it whenever she felt worried. But Elric was more important than honey. She had carried him to this safe place and made a fire. She needed him to get better, and now he was. She did well.

She wouldn't lose him like Mother.

Elric was quiet. He didn't seem very happy. His face didn't look like it normally did, and the purple spots looked bad. He didn't say much when Wynn hummed her song. All he did was turn his knife over and over in his hands.

"Come here," he said. Wynn was glad to hear him speak, but he didn't sound right. His voice came out like he was angry, but he should be glad. He was getting better now. Wynn did as she was told and walked over to him, scratching the dried mud near her ear. He hung his head as if it were aching, then looked up at her without a smile. "I need to cut your hair."

Cut her hair? Why? Mother had never cut her hair. Wynn immediately backed up. "No!"

Elric's eyes were dark from bruises and nearly swollen shut. They looked squinting and angry. The scab on his cut lip quivered as his mouth turned down. "You ruined your skirt. Now you're dressed like a boy. You might as well look like one so you blend in. We can't afford to attract any more attention from people who might hurt us."

"I don't want to be a boy," she said, shaking her head.

"You won't be a boy. You'll just look like one. It's for your own good. Now come here." He motioned to her, but he wasn't looking at her. He was looking at all their things and picking clothes up to put in his sack. He seemed worried, but she didn't want to cut her hair.

"No." Wynn stumbled on the rocks near her fire.

"Wynn, now is not the time to be stubborn. I know what I'm doing. Hold still. I don't want to cut you." Elric grabbed her by the arm. She pulled but he held on. His grip hurt her. Wynn's heart raced as she threw her weight back. Her shoulder ached, and she twisted her elbow. She had to get away.

He let go suddenly and she fell to the ground. It knocked the wind out of her. She twisted over to try to get up, but he climbed on her the way he did when shearing a sheep. He sat on her back so she couldn't push herself free. "Get off me!" she shouted. Chunks of moss got into her mouth, tasting bitter and gritty in her teeth. Bits of dirt went up her nose and stung. Her nose started running, and she couldn't pull in air. "Stop!"

"I'm sorry, but you can't even take care of it. It will be easier this way," Elric said, sounding both frustrated and pleading.

Her hair was pretty. It was the color of the fields when the sun was shining and people were happy. Mother brushed it every night. It was hers. He couldn't take it from her. She thrashed her head.

"I told you, hold still. I don't want to hurt you!" Elric's fist tightened on her braid. Her scalp stung where he pulled it.

No! No! No!

She kicked; she pushed against the ground, but his weight was too much for her.

She felt the knife like a saw, cutting. "Stop it!" she screamed.

Tears spilled out of her eyes. She reached back, clawing at his legs, wanting to hurt him. A lock of her hair fell against her cheek. It was broken.

The knife sawed and sawed.

"Stop it!" she cried, choking on her sob.

"Don't worry, I'm almost done," Elric said, as if nothing were wrong. The tension holding her head back released, and her face fell forward onto the damp moss. It was gone.

"There, that looks a lot better," Elric said as he climbed off her back, but she couldn't move. Wynn cried. She reached a hand up to her hair, but instead of the long thick braid, her hair slithered through her fingers for only a moment before her hand came away, and there was nothing.

Tears poured out of her eyes. She couldn't speak. It was gone, and her heart hurt. Her heart hurt so badly.

"Get up, Wynn. Don't be a baby." His voice sounded rough. It didn't sound like his voice. She heard Elric's footsteps but she didn't look at him. She couldn't look at him. "It's only hair. It will grow back."

Slowly she pushed herself up just enough that she could curl into a little ball. Her stomach hurt, like she was sick. She couldn't breathe. Her words wouldn't come. It was gone.

"Mine," she said through her sobs. The word rang through the clearing. She lifted her head, chunks of her now-chin-length hair falling into her face. She tried to push them away, but they fell back. In her frustration she grabbed them and pulled hard as she screamed. She shrieked louder and louder until Elric covered his ears.

"Wynn, stop it! It's only hair!" Elric tried to force her hands away from her scalp, but she threw her arm hard and jabbed her elbow into his side. He cried out and fell away from her.

She stood. "Pretty!" she shouted at him. It was the only part of her that was pretty. Mother liked to brush it. She would brush it by the fire and say, "Such pretty hair for my pretty girl." And Wynn felt proud. Now it was gone.

Elric's eyes were wide, even though they were swollen. She had never seen him like this. Maybe he wasn't really her brother at all. Maybe he had been changed into a monster. "I had to cut it!" Elric shouted. "I already told you. Your dress looks like a tunic. And if you look like a boy, no one will notice you. That will help keep us safe. Besides, it's clean now that I cut the mud out of it. Pack our things. It's time to go."

"NO!" Wynn balled her hands into fists. "I don't like you anymore."

Her tears dripped from her chin, and water ran from her nose. She helped him. He hurt her.

Wynn turned and ran.

The trees flew past, but she couldn't see them. She couldn't see anything through her tears. There was no doe to lead her, only her feet. She ran as fast as she could. She wanted to run from him forever.

"Wynn!" he called, but his voice was far away already. "Wynn, come back!"

No!

She ran.

The forest streamed by with branches reaching out to scratch at her as she passed. She didn't care. They didn't hurt her. A pain stabbed in her heart, and it forced her to slow. Her breath came in aching bursts. When she couldn't run, she stumbled, then found her strength and ran again. Her shorn hair fell into her eyes over and over. She brushed it away with slashing hands, feeling her nails scratch her own face.

It didn't matter where she was going. There were no sticks to guide her. She would never find Elric again.

She didn't care.

She no longer heard his voice. She no longer had the strength to run. She fell to her knees near the stump of a tree and cried.

She couldn't stop crying.

Wynn sat against the stump and pulled her legs tight against her chest. It was starting to feel cold. She left her cloak with *him*. She wouldn't go back. He was supposed to be the brother who laughed with her and played games. She wanted the brother who wrapped her in big hugs when he came home from the fields. She didn't want this. She rubbed a hand over her bare neck. The fringes of her chopped hair tickled her palm.

This wasn't a game anymore.

It was hard for Wynn to remember things if she didn't think about them over and over. Things that happened didn't stay in her mind well. Now she couldn't brush her hair and remember when Mother did it. She would forget. She always forgot.

Wrapping her arms around her knees, she let her face press against them. Tufts of her hair fell forward in a fringe around her eyes. Her tongue stuck to the roof of her mouth and her tummy grumbled.

She was alone.

Good.

She didn't want to be with anyone.

She was cold.

She was sad.

She was hungry.

Now what was she going to do?

She opened her mouth, but she couldn't sing. Instead she coughed out another painful sob and curled tighter in on herself. The shadows of the trees wavered in the wind. To Wynn, they looked like a hand reaching for her.

She didn't know how long she sat there.

It didn't matter.

Something rustled nearby.

A little hope came back to her.

"Mildred?" she called, though it hurt to speak. Her hen always managed to follow her.

"What are you doing out here alone?" a man's voice asked. She didn't recognize it.

Wynn snapped her head up and scurried to the other side of the hacked-off stump.

He came closer.

CHAPTER TWELVE

Elric

ELRIC STOOD WITH WYNN'S SEVERED braid in his hand. He didn't know how long he had been there, staring at the limp rope of hair crossing his palm. What had he done? He clenched his fist on the soft hair. He did what he had to do.

Elric dropped the braid on the ground.

Stomping around the clearing he yanked the various pieces of clothing and supplies he had gathered and shoved them forcefully back in his sack even though his bruises ached. Now he would have to go find her. It was one more bother he'd have to deal with because she didn't understand what was going on.

He came to the empty jar of honey and picked it up. The crushed remains of the herbs she had shoved in her sack lay scattered beneath his feet. Elric sighed.

The only thing useful she had packed was the pot. He kicked it off the fire. The boiling water fell over the hot coals with an angry hiss and a cloud of white smoke curled up into the cool spring air.

Awwwk . . . bok . . . bok . . .

Mildred scratched at the trampled herbs, then peered up at him with one fiery eye.

"What are you looking at?" He shoved the empty honey jar into his sack.

The hen shook her comb at him, the curve of her beak giving her a wary frown.

"This is not my fault," he reasoned. "Wynn gets too worked up over silly things. And she was being stubborn."

The hen clucked low in her throat, the sound remarkably like a dismissive *tut, tut.*

Great. The last thing he needed was a know-it-all hen. "She makes a mess of things. I'm lucky I wasn't killed last night. I was trying to save her and this is the thanks I get." He pointed to his bruised and swollen face. "Now I have to go tromping off through the woods to who-knows-where to find her. Then when I do, she'll be impossible to deal with." Elric sat down on a rock and let his face rest in his hands, but the touch of his palms on his bruised jaw hurt too badly. He let his hands drop and sighed.

Mildred stepped over to him, her head bobbing as she did.

"It's hard," he admitted. "No one knows how hard this is. I remember the nights Mother cried because it was late, and she was tired, but she had to clean underclothes again and again and again because Wynn had soiled them like a baby. Mother always looked worn. And now I'm so tired. I'm trying to care for her. I'm doing the best I can."

Elric ran his hand over Mildred's broad back. The light caught on the deep-brown spots and streaks in her dark feathers. "Mother should have had someone who could help her. She only had me, and I had to go tend the sheep. I left them alone too much. If I had been there, I would have noticed Mother's illness. I could have helped."

Mother was gone. Wynn was now his responsibility.

He never chose this. She wasn't his child. He didn't choose to be her brother. This was something that had been thrust upon him, and it had given him nothing but trouble for his efforts. His lip stung, and he dabbed at the scabby cut there that tasted like honey.

All he wanted was to return to his home—even if that life was oppressive, at least it was predictable. He could raise the sheep, take over Father's house in the hamlet one day. He'd inherit responsibility for his father's lands, and glean as much as he could from them. Perhaps he would find a wife and have sons that could help him work off the debts he would owe to the church and their lord.

It's what everyone else did. It is what they had all done for generations.

He closed his eyes and tried to picture his mother. He could picture her smiling as Wynn clung to her apron until given a hug. Or her sitting near Wynn as his sister slept, softly smoothing back her daughter's hair and singing.

Elric looked down at the severed braid near his feet. He picked it up gently. The braid began to unwind in his hand, and he quickly separated the strands so he could weave it back together tighter. He tied off the severed end with a bit of torn fabric, then brushed away the mud and pulled out the twigs that had caught in it.

He worked one of the sharp blackthorns out of the braid and held it to the light. What was he doing? He couldn't leave Wynn alone out here. She'd never survive on her own.

He had made a promise.

Tuck . . . tuck . . . tuck . . . Mildred pecked his toe with a sharp jab of her beak.

"Ow!" Elric jumped to his feet as the hen threatened to peck him again. "Enough! I hear you!" He dodged out of the angry hen's path and looped the severed rope of hair in the belt tied around his waist. "I have to go find her."

He packed away the cooled pot and picked up Wynn's empty sack. He slung it over his shoulder, then swung the heavy sack up. The strap dug into his bruises. He tried to shift it, but nothing helped. Mildred watched him intently, her beak open and ready to peck him again.

He looked up toward the surrounding trees and realized he was only vaguely aware of which direction Wynn had run.

"You wouldn't happen to know which way she went, would you?" Elric said to the fat hen, not expecting an answer. To his surprise, the chicken fluffed out her feathers, then strutted confidently across the mossy clearing and through the strange circle of rocks. With head and tail high, and comb bobbing merrily, she marched forward.

Elric followed her, feeling completely foolish as he did so. She was a chicken—a stupid bird couldn't find a lost girl in the woods. But he supposed it was as good a direction as any.

Mildred trotted on, hopping over large rocks with a flap of her broad wings, and striding confidently through the thick trees and deep shadows of the forest. She didn't stop to scratch or peck at the dead leaves. Instead her beak pointed straight as an arrow down the path.

The shadows grew, casting the forest in a strange twilight beneath the branches, and Elric started to worry.

Wynn was probably so scared. He'd find her cold, hungry, and miserable. As soon as he built a fire and scavenged something to eat, all would be forgiven.

He'd have to explain to her, yet again, the dangers of wandering too far off, and hope that this time his words remained in her mind.

"Wynn!" he called.

His own stomach growled.

They didn't have anything left to eat.

"Wynn?" He tried again. "Don't fret, I'm not mad at you."

A sick feeling twisted through his gut, and it had nothing to do with his hunger.

What if he couldn't find her?

His sister would starve out here alone. She'd have no way to find food, or build shelter. She could barely start a fire, and even if she had any talent at it, he had the flint in his pack.

It wouldn't take her long to die of thirst, or illness from drinking foul water. She wouldn't know how to tell if water was clean.

He picked up his feet as he jogged with greater purpose through the ominous woods. What if she ate berries that were poisonous?

Mildred let out a high-pitched squawk as Elric nearly kicked her in his haste. She flapped ahead, then ran, her wide body rolling with the motion of her striding legs.

Elric stopped in his tracks as he came to a high bank.

What if someone else found her first? Someone who wanted to hurt her?

"Wynn!" he shouted, his voice tinged with panic.

He threw himself up the embankment, digging his sore hands into the loose dirt to cling to the roots from the trees above. Dirt rained down on his face, and he spit it out from between his lips. His shoulders strained, and his ribs ached, but he gritted his teeth and pushed hard with his legs to launch his upper body over the top of the ridge.

He landed hard on his ribs and grunted in pain. Pulling himself up, he rolled on the ground holding his middle. Mildred flapped furiously as she struggled to the top of the embankment.

Gasping, he opened his eyes. A nearby stump bore a rough-chopped wedge and jaggedly broken wood on top. The tree had been cut down with an ax.

The comforting aroma of a wood fire sent a chill down his spine. Someone lived nearby.

Elric kept a hand on his ribs as he used the other one to push himself up into a cautious crouch. He shrugged the sack off his shoulder.

"Millie, come here," he whispered.

The hen took a slow step toward him. He gently scooped her up and placed her in the sack. She tried to poke her head out, but he tucked it down and drew the string tight.

A twig snapped behind him.

He whipped himself up to his full height, pulling his knife out of his belt as he did so.

"Back away!" he shouted, only to take a shocked step backward. He nearly slid down the embankment.

The jester from the village stood on the felled tree near the chopped stump wearing normal clothing instead of colorful rags. He crossed his wrists over the blunt end of the handle of an ax that was nearly as large as he was.

"Why should I back away?" The man gave Elric an incredulous smile. "You're the fool who stumbled on my land."

CHAPTER THIRTEEN
Elric

ELRIC TUCKED HIS KNIFE BACK in his belt. "It's only you."

The jester touched his forehead as if it pained him and sighed. "Are you certain you want to put that away? I am holding an ax."

Elric chuckled as he leaned against a tree. "I'll take my chances."

"Figures you wouldn't be any different from the others." The jester shook his head sadly. Without another word he turned and walked along the top of the fallen log. "Save your thick-headed arrogance for someone else."

It took a moment for the man's words to sink in. When they did, shame filled his heart. At the same time he realized that the presence of a somewhat familiar face had made the forest seem less intimidating. Now the prospect of being alone worried him. He jogged along the side of the fallen tree to catch up with the man. "Wait, I could use your help," Elric called, ducking under a thick limb. Maybe he had seen Wynn.

"I have no use for you," he said.

"I'm looking for my sister." Elric peered around the clearing and at every turn, the forest seemed overgrown and deep with shadows.

"Maybe your sister has no use for you either." He hopped off the felled tree and ran his hand over one of the thicker branches.

"My sister can't survive without me," Elric said, keeping close to the trunk of the tree. Mildred let out a series of clucks that sounded suspiciously like laughter.

"And yet, you are searching for her, but she is not searching for you." The dwarf hitched up his sleeves and swung his ax. He swept it up and over in a masterful arc that fell with precision against the branch. Elric flinched as the ax hit the branch with a heavy *thunk* that betrayed the strength of the swing. The man levered the handle to release the blade and swung again. The branch snapped off in only two strokes, and the man tossed it onto a large stack of freshly cut wood. Elric shuddered as he realized he had greatly misjudged the man's strength. Perhaps he shouldn't have put his knife away.

"Listen, my sister is a half-wit and she doesn't know what's good for her." Elric reached down and picked up a cut length of wood that had tumbled off the pile, and placed it back on the stack.

"And you do?" The jester shook a wood chip out of his thick mop of dusty brown hair.

Elric was used to spending several days at a time wandering through the countryside with the flock. Wynn was helpless out here. "Of course I do."

It was the jester's turn to laugh. "What's your name, son?"

"Elric."

The man crossed his stocky arms. "And who am I?"

Well, that was obvious. There weren't many men around of his stature. "You're the fool from the village."

He swung the ax hard, and it lodged deep in the trunk. Then he picked up three of the logs from the pile and walked away. "Like I said, I have no use for you."

Elric's mind spun. He wasn't sure what the man wanted from him. "Wait!"

"Why? You have given me no reason to." The jester kept walking toward a stout hut in the distance. Elric ran to catch up. The hut was much smaller than he had first thought. It had been built from the thick branches of old trees, with stacked wood and mud forming the walls and windows between. A dense blanket of shaggy grass covered the roof, and the jester's hairy gray goat happily grazed on it. She bleated in greeting and the door opened.

"Osmund?" Wynn ducked under the low door, pushing her chin-length hair behind her ear. "The stew is ready."

"Wynnfrith!" Elric ran to her, but she retreated into the house and slammed the crooked door in his face. Elric came up short and stumbled backward.

"Well now, that wasn't a very warm welcome, was it?" the jester commented.

"Why didn't you tell me she was here?" Elric rounded on the man even as his head rushed with relief. Wynn was safe.

Osmund smiled and leaned back against the rough

wall of his hut. "Because she told me she didn't want to see you, and I took her at her word."

Elric slid the two sacks off his shoulder. Mildred squawked and struggled out of the top one. She immediately fluffed her feathers, then pecked his toe with a sharp jab of her beak.

"Ow, Mildred!" Elric hopped on one foot as the hen trotted toward the hut. "You ungrateful sack of feathers!" The hen paused and cocked her head at him. The angle made her comb dangle in a way that gave her a haughty expression. She shook out her tail, then strutted toward the hut. One of Wynn's eyes appeared briefly in the window, then sank back into the dark interior.

Mildred took a running leap, flapped her wings, and perched on the sill. Wynn's hands slowly emerged from the window and pulled the hen inside.

"Come out, Wynn," Elric called through the door. "It's time to leave."

"Where are you going to go?" Osmund asked, picking at his fingernails.

"It doesn't matter." Elric pushed a hand through the front of his hair, and it stuck on the dried honey.

"Then why are you in a hurry?" The goat wandered down from the roof, hopping on an embankment running along the back of the house. She bleated as she reached her master, and Osmond pet her rounded ears.

"I don't know," he whispered. "We have no place left to go." Elric felt every ache and pain in his body. He closed his burning eyes and let his head hang for a moment. He was tired. He hurt. He was hungry. He needed help. But he didn't want to admit any of that.

Osmond walked past him and opened the door, the goat trotted in. "Come inside, son."

Elric had to bend to tuck himself through the small door. The inside of the hut was dark, but comfortable and surprisingly warm. A large fire blazed in a stone hearth, while a small bed, short log stools, and a low table filled the single room.

Wynn sat cross-legged in the corner with Mildred nestled in her lap. She took one look at him and turned to face the wall.

"Don't be cross," Elric said as he sat on one of the squat logs. His knees rose too high in front of him and he felt comically awkward, like some giant that couldn't squeeze himself into a normal-size house. He'd never been in a place that wasn't built for him, and it made him deeply uncomfortable.

"Your sister has every right to be angry. If you don't

see that, then you are the one who is having trouble *here*." Osmund tapped his temple with one finger. He sat in a chair that had been hewn out of an old stump, kicking his feet up on an overturned bucket. An amulet fell out of the neck of his shirt. He tucked it out of view quickly, but not before Elric caught a glimpse of a strange pattern that looked like a flower with three petals.

"All I did was . . ."

"I know what you did. I'm more interested in what you didn't do," Osmund said. He placed his hands behind his head. The goat kneeled beside him, then flopped on its side like a dog laying at its master's feet.

"What do you mean, *what I didn't do*?" Elric's stomach growled. The savory roasted-onion scent of the stew filled the small hut and made his mouth water. They hadn't had real food in days. Wynn hiccupped in the corner, but didn't turn around. "You don't even know what happened."

"I know you told a man on the road that you needed to buy a pig." Osmund rubbed his knee as if it were hurting him. "I know that Wynn tried to help. I know that people can be cruel. I know that I humiliated myself to distract those boys and save you both from trouble. I know trouble found you anyway. I know your sister, in spite of the dark, in spite of the danger, went back for you and carried you to safety. I know she spent all night cleaning your things and healing your wounds."

"She poured honey on them," Elric complained. "She made a mess of things."

"Honey keeps wounds from festering." His voice took on a sharp edge. "Pouring honey on those cuts saved your life, and what did you do?"

Elric hung his head. He didn't feel like eating anymore.

"You wounded her," Osmund finished.

"I was careful not to hurt her, even though she wouldn't hold still," Elric said. Wynn's hiccups grew louder, or was she crying again?

"Not all wounds bleed." Osmund stood and hobbled over to the fire. He scooped the bubbling stew from the pot onto a wooden trencher and handed it to Wynn. "Careful, it's hot," he said to her. Then he turned back to Elric, "But like I said, I'm more interested in what you didn't do."

"What was I supposed to do? None of this is my fault." Elric pushed his heel out and banged his shin on the low table. "Her only dress is ruined, and she'd draw even more attention to herself walking around in a boy's clothing. I had to disguise her."

Osmund laughed as he filled another trencher with food. "And you called *me* the fool. I give up. Here, eat."

Elric was hungry enough to shove the stew as quickly as he could into his mouth. It looked tender and filled his senses with the fresh scent of wild herbs and hot broth. But his stomach was turning over and over.

He didn't understand what Osmund was asking of him. His head hurt just thinking about it. Was he supposed to feel bad? He did what he had to do. Osmund didn't say anything for a while, and it made Elric uncomfortable, like he had to fill the silence.

"Why do you do it?" Elric asked, catching Osmund in the midst of lifting the turnip he had stabbed with a short knife to his lips.

"Eat?" he asked.

"No, play the fool in the village," Elric said. Osmund's mind was like a snare. Elric didn't want to get caught in the trap of it again. Why would an intelligent man want to throw himself in the mud and ride on a goat? It didn't make any sense.

"It's a job. What else does this world allow me to be?" Osmund responded. "Do I get to be a knight, valiant and brave? I'm sure one day I'll be called to ride off on a noble steed to save a fair princess from a dragon."

Elric choked on a turnip, and the goat bleated, then closed her eyes again.

"I think you're a knight," Wynn said from her spot next to the wall. "You are very kind. You help."

Osmund smiled at her. "Will you be my princess fair, Wynnfrith?"

She scrunched her nose. "No."

"No?" He raised an eyebrow at her.

"I want to be the dragon," Wynn said as she let Mildred peck at her empty trencher.

Osmund let out a hearty laugh, and Elric smiled. That was like Wynn. Half the time they played, she wanted to run from the Grendel, the other half, she wanted to pretend to be the Grendel's mother and eat people.

"I don't get to choose how people see me," Osmund said, his voice bitter as he watched Wynn stroke the hen's back. "No one cares if I am a good wood-carver, or goatherd, or farmer. No one seems to notice that I can build things, fix things, hunt things. They look at me, and they see only one part of me. One purpose. They will laugh whether I want them to or not. So I make them laugh."

Elric shifted in his seat, unsure what to say. He had laughed too, when he met Osmund in the woods and underestimated his strength.

"No matter how much you try to hide her, or change her, people will still see what they want to see," Osmund added in a softer voice. "They will see her, and do what they will. That is not her fault."

"So there is no place that is safe for us," Elric muttered. He watched his sister smile as she scooped up her hen in her arms and buried her face into the feathers of the bird's back.

Osmund looked him in the eye. "Not in this world."

Elric shook his head. "We can't change the world, and there is no other one."

"There's the court of the Fairy Queen," Wynn said. "She's through the Silver Gate."

Surprised that she had spoken, Elric turned to her. "That's just a song."

She frowned as if she were terribly disappointed in him.

"Osmund?" Elric crossed his arms. "Could you please tell her that some things are nothing more than fanciful tales for children?"

Osmund picked up the trenchers with a strange look

in his eyes. He had gone slightly pale, as if he'd seen a ghost. His hand came to the center of his chest, touching the amulet hidden there. He shook his head as if clearing his thoughts, then said to Wynn, "From one changeling to another, don't believe everything you are told."

"That's sound advice." Elric tried to stretch out his legs, but they would have blocked half the room.

"I don't believe you, Elric," Wynn stated quite clearly. "The Fairy Queen is real."

Osmund dropped the wooden trenchers into a bucket of water. His hands were shaking. He clenched them quickly when he noticed Elric watching them.

Elric had an uneasy feeling, but turned his attention back to his sister. "Have you ever seen the Fairy Queen?" Elric asked. Osmund sat down, his attention completely focused on Wynn's answer.

"She hears me when I sing." Wynn stroked Mildred's neck, and the bird seemed to nod in agreement.

"How can you know that?" Elric protested.

"I know it," Wynn said. Mildred clucked beside her, and the goat let out an encouraging bleat.

Elric rolled his eyes and decided to humor her. "Fine, even if she were real, finding her court would be impossible. We'd have to travel north until we found the

White Mountain, across wood and moor. Then the only way to see the Silver Gate is if she somehow magically decides to gift us with her silver staff. That's not likely to happen."

"It can," Wynn insisted.

"How do you know about the staff?" Osmund asked, his tone urgent.

Elric turned to the man. "How do *you* know about the staff?" he asked. The Silver Gate was a silly song and story their mother had made up to keep them busy when they were young. There was no truth to it.

"Just tell me." Osmund nearly overturned a clay cup by his hand. His hands were shaking worse now.

"It's a song. Mother would sing it for us," Elric confessed, gripping the spoon in his belt. He looked down at it. At one time, it was a sword that could slay the foulest beast. It was an ax that could hew the largest tree. It was the silver staff and an archer's bow. It was everything he was when he was young and life was full of fairy tales. It was all he needed to reach the Silver Gate. Now as he looked at it, all he could see was a spoon.

Wynn began to sing.

To Elric's surprise, Osmund's voice joined Wynn's. His voice carried over hers, guiding hers back on key as he sang the tune by heart. When they reached the end of the song, Wynn clapped wildly and the goat bleat in approval. "You are a very good singer," Wynn said.

Osmund gave her a quick bow. "Thank you, as are you. I have known that melody from the time I was a small babe. I didn't think I would ever hear it again. How did your mother come to know it?"

"It's just a song," Elric protested, though he was equally curious how Osmund had learned it. It was probably the work of some traveling bard who sang the tune on market day. There couldn't be anything more to it. He tapped the spoon against his knee.

"That is not just a song," Osmund said as he stood and walked to the fire. He watched the flames dancing over the burning logs and crossed his arms. "Many hundreds of years ago, Queen Mab could travel to and from our world with ease through the Silver Gate. Her magic was endless, and she could make fairy circles appear wherever she wished. In those years, the weather was fairer, game was abundant, and good fortune came to all those who asked for her favor."

Wynn scooted closer to Osmund to hear his tale. Elric rubbed his forehead, knowing he would never get silly notions out of her head now.

"What happened next?" Wynn asked.

"The queen gave birth to a child, a child she marked to lead her armies against the greatest darkness to threaten her fairy realm, the Grendel."

Wynn clutched Mildred tighter. The hen gave a loud squawk of protest.

Elric knew the Grendel would come into the story somewhere. "Let me guess, he snuck into the fairy villages and ate the villagers," Elric mumbled.

Osmund gave him a look as grave as an executioner. "Worse. I cannot even speak of the terror of it. He comes with the force of a terrible storm, or hides lurking in silent shadows. The darkness that surrounds him is tangible. It feels like a thick oil on your skin. He feeds on all that is good in a person and leaves nothing but anger and hatred in the hole he leaves in your spirit. He can corrupt the purest heart and turn a good creature into a monster. But the Grendel could not enter the borders of the Fairy Queen's realm. With the birth of her child, the queen became even more powerful, capable of drawing on the love of her child and turning it into a force she could wield like a weapon. The power of the queen's magic nearly defeated the Grendel. But he was crafty. One night he corrupted some creatures from the

Darkling Wood on the borders of the queen's realm. They snuck into the heart of the palace and crept into the nursery. Cloaked by the shadows of the Grendel's power, they stole the baby."

"No," Wynn whispered, looking stricken. Osmund gave her a nod.

"With the loss of her child, the queen succumbed to terrible grief. Her heart broke, and when it did, her power waned. It hasn't fully returned since. For the past hundred years, she's had only the power to shield her people. Now the Grendel lurks, waiting for his chance to strike and cover all the land Between in darkness."

"Don't listen to this, Wynn, it's only stories," Elric said.

Wynn glanced at him, then peered up at Osmund with wonder shining in her eyes. "Can we stay with you?" she asked him. He rose and closed a leather flap over the window.

"I'm sorry," he said to Wynn. "I would love to be your knight and save you from this place. But I built this hut for me and Burghild, my goat. You can't even stand straight in it." He turned to Elric. "And you've made some enemies in the village. Don't think for a minute they won't talk, or rally to have you both thrown in the stocks until someone can bring you back to your own village for reckoning. If they know I helped you, they'd put me in the stocks just to see my feet dangle."

"Then we can't stay," Elric said. "We don't want to cause any more trouble for you."

"I'm sorry I can't be more of a help." Osmund shook his head sadly. "I know how it feels to find yourself suddenly alone and lost in this world. Besides, it's nice having guests, even ones who eat me out of half my stores."

"Thank you, Osmund." Elric hesitated, hoping Osmund could hear that he meant his words this time and they were from the heart. "For everything you've done for us, especially Wynn. You're a good man."

Osmund's face softened. "Now you're learning. Get some sleep."

Wynn and Elric settled down near the fire. Elric had to push the table closer to Osmund's bed just to get enough room to curl up into a ball. To his dismay, Burghild the goat decided to lie down right next to him. As the fire died, Osmund began to snore.

Elric had a lot to think about. They would have to keep traveling to stay away from anyone who might suspect they were breaking bonds of fealty, and hope they passed beyond the reach of their lord. Maybe they would have better luck in a faraway village and find another kind person to help. At least Osmund proved there were generous people in the world.

He looked over at his sister, her hastily sliced hair falling in uneven chunks across the soft dirt floor.

"Wynn?"

She didn't move, but Elric knew she could hear him. She always rolled onto her back and splayed her arms and legs out if she was really asleep.

He wanted to say something to her, but he didn't know what. He didn't know how to explain what he had to do in a way she would understand and accept. "Don't worry," he said. "Things will be better in the morning."

She took a deep breath.

Wynn remained silent, and Elric didn't say anything more. Instead he stayed awake watching the burning embers of the fire slowly die.

The next morning, Osmund helped load their sacks with heavy bread, goat cheese, chunks of dried meat, turnips, parsnips, carrots, and a couple of onions. He also filled the honey jar and gave them two bladders, one filled with water, and the other with goat's milk. He gave Elric a snare for birds and rabbits, and a small ax. It was rusted and the handle split down the grain of the wood, but it was a generous gift all the same.

"Good luck," he said as he tied the second sack and handed it to Wynn. "I hope you do find a place that is safe for you."

Wynn dropped the sack at her feet and bent to give the man a very big hug. He patted her on the back. "Stay fierce, Wynn the Dragon."

"Come with me." Wynn didn't let go.

"I'm sorry, my dear, I wish I could, but who would look after Burghild?"

"She is a good goat." Slowly Wynn let go and pulled on a cap Osmund had given her, woven from his goat's hair.

"You take care of that hen of yours," Osmund said. "The smart ones are worth keeping." Mildred trotted across the garden on the trail of a fat beetle. Osmund motioned to Elric as he straightened with the heavy sack on his bruised shoulder. It ached as the strap cut into it, but there were worse forms of torture, so he'd have to bear it. A heavy sack was better than an empty one.

Osmund scooped up Mildred, and placed the hen in

Wynn's arms. "Thank you for all your help around the house," he said to her. "That was the best rabbit stew I've ever had."

Wynn giggled. "Welcome."

He gave her a deep bow. "I hope that one day our paths may cross again, fair Wynnfrith the Dragon. Until then, go with your brother."

Wynn looked up at him, and a stern frown drew her eyebrows down. It wasn't an expression she was used to making, and it crumpled up her face unnaturally.

"I can take care of myself," she insisted.

Osmund leaned in toward her. "Then take care of him. He will get it eventually," Osmund murmured as he gave her shoulder a strong pat. "He doesn't understand things the way we do." He turned back toward Elric. "A word?"

Elric nodded.

Osmund led him over to the embankment behind the house. "Listen, I don't know where you intend to go, but no matter how desperate you get, do not seek the Silver Gate. You will never find it."

Elric stared at him. "You believe it exists?"

"Would you seek it if it does?" Osmund asked.

"You didn't answer my question," Elric said, gripping

the handle of his mother's spoon. "You know something. Something you're not telling me."

Osmund pulled Elric down so he could speak eye to eye. "It doesn't matter if I believe. What matters is what *you* believe." He patted Elric on the shoulder and turned back to his hut without another word.

CHAPTER FOURTEEN

Elric

THEIR PATH LED NORTH, AND it was as good as any at the moment as long as it led them far away from the village. The last thing they needed was more trouble. Wynn skipped along the path, gathering the new buds of early spring wildflowers. "Wynn, stay behind me," Elric groused. "You don't know the way."

Her smile faded, and with hunched shoulders, she fell into step behind him.

With her eyes narrowed, she crossed her arms. He marched forward and Wynn kicked up leaves behind him. At least she was walking in peace through the woods without her incessant singing.

He could hear himself think, and also hear if any trouble was coming.

They walked the full day and she hardly said a word.

Mildred was also unnaturally quiet as she hunted bugs in the new spring shoots pushing up through the thick layer of dried grasses. Every time the hen passed by him, she stared at him through one red-and-gold pupil. She was thinking about pecking him, he knew it. Sure enough, she jabbed her beak at his toe every chance she got.

The second day was silent as well. While they managed to travel several miles, by the end of the evening, Elric was feeling half mad. He was used to going for days on end without anyone to speak to while tending the sheep, but this was different.

It was strange to have someone following only steps behind him without saying a word. It was unnatural, especially for Wynn, and it made him uncomfortable. As evening fell, he tried talking with Mildred, just to hear a voice even if it was only his own. The hen seemed intent upon ignoring him completely too.

On the third day, after hiking through steadily

rising hills all afternoon, and as the sun was beginning to set, he finally broke.

"Wynn, I had to cut your hair. Remember when we passed that shepherd? He just waved at us without even looking at you. The disguise is working, so you have no right to be angry with me anymore." Elric let his sack fall to the ground in a cluster of old oak trees. Their branches twisted and tangled like black snakes trying to slither into a red-and-orange sky. He turned to Wynn. She just gently let her sack down and lifted Mildred out of it, so the hen could scratch through the leaves.

But she still didn't say anything.

"Fine, I'll keep ignoring you then," Elric said. "See if it makes any difference to me." He pulled out the small pot and the wooden spoon, then took up the ax and eyed the trees for a broken limb that might be dry enough to cut for a fire.

The pot clanked behind him.

Elric turned around, and Wynn was holding the wooden spoon.

He rushed back toward her. "Don't touch that!"

She immediately pulled the spoon in toward her chest and twisted away from him, cowering as if he were about to strike her.

He realized he was holding the ax.

Slowly Elric dropped it to the soft ground. "Just give me the spoon." He held his hand out to her.

"Why?" her voice sounded hoarse from lack of use.

"It was Mother's." Elric took another quick step toward her, but she shied away again, still clutching the spoon. "I don't want you to break it."

Elric's heart pounded faster and faster. A sweat broke out on his brow. It was all he had left of Mother. He knew it was silly, but when he held the whittled shaft of the spoon in his hand, he remembered what it was like to be carefree.

He remembered the earthy smell of his mother's dress as he pressed his face into it as a little boy while her arms wrapped around him. For a moment, he remembered how it felt to be cared for when his world was safe and warm.

Wynn looked at the spoon. "This is my spoon," she said. "I use it for cooking."

"No it's not," he said. "Give it back to me, now!"

He lunged at Wynn, but she ran with surprising speed. Elric chased her, accidentally kicking Mildred as the hen ran after them both. He looked down at the bird and stumbled over her just enough to throw himself off balance. Mildred flew in another direction, clucking angrily as her wings flapped at her sides.

His shoulder hit the dried leaves and the layer of lumpy and shifting acorns covering the ground. He scrambled to get back up, but the balls of his feet slipped on the acorns.

By the time he finally got his feet under him, Wynn had sprinted far ahead of him. Her gait was awkward but she was fast in spite of it. Elric's lungs burned as he fought to catch up with her.

He tasted blood in his mouth, and he didn't care.

He had to get that spoon back.

Elric bent and scooped up a handful of acorns. With a quick flick of his wrist, he hurled them at his sister.

One hit her in the back of the head.

"Ow!" She stopped running for a second and reached up to rub her head. It knocked the hat Osmund had given her askew.

Elric pushed his sore legs harder. He was gaining on her now.

She caught sight of him, let out a squeak, and turned to run. The hat fell from her head, and her short hair flew behind her as she took off again.

Elric heaved in several breaths. Wynn had never run this fast before.

Of course, she'd always been wearing a long dress before.

A cramp pinched his side. He held it as he flew past tree trunk after tree trunk. Wynn stumbled, and he was on her.

He leaped at her, grasping for the spoon. They tumbled down a small hill, the fallen leaves flying around them as they fought.

"Stop it!" Elric shouted at her, grabbing at her arms. She whacked him several times over the head with the spoon, each strike ringing in his skull and leaving a sharp, lingering pain in his scalp.

He got a hand on the handle of the spoon and used it to push one of Wynn's hands off. She immediately grabbed it again, kicking at him. "It's not yours, let go!" Elric shouted.

"It's mine!" Wynn screeched, the dried oak leaves embedding themselves in her knife-cut hair.

Elric tightened his fist on the spoon and tried to peel her fingers off the handle, but she bent her short thumbs straight backward, her fingers flexing in unnatural ways. Every time he got one hand free, she grabbed the handle again.

"Enough!" Elric yanked hard and heard a loud snap.

His heart stopped in that moment.

Wynn went still.

The spoon came away from her hands cracked in two.

Wynn pushed away from him, her bright blue eyes wide with fear as she stared at him.

He looked down at the broken pieces of the spoon, one in each of his open palms. He closed his fingers over them, feeling the delicate wood across his hardening fists. He staggered to his feet.

"What have you done?" he screamed at Wynn.

She cowered beneath him, half buried in the leaves; her tangled hair covered her face as she stared up at him. "I didn't mean to."

"You broke it!" The words ripped out of his chest so hard they burned. Wynn covered her ears, and a tear spilled over her cheek.

"I'm sorry," she said.

Elric aligned the two pieces, watching the splintered wood come together. When he pressed, it was as if it had never broken at all. But then he let go, and it fell in two.

He threw both pieces at Wynn.

"I'm done with you." He dusted the leaves off his heavy tunic. "I can't do this anymore. I'm going home."

He stomped back through the forest, the leaves and twigs crunching under his feet. He could feel each lump through the worn soles of his shoes. They hurt. He hurt. He had a deep pain in his chest, and he still was breathless from fighting.

His skin itched all over as he tried to brush the bits of leaves and dirt that had crawled into his clothes away from his skin. It didn't work.

The fiery colors in the sky faded into the softer gray of twilight.

He reached the grove where his sack, the pot, and a ruffled Mildred still waited. He gathered up his things, throwing them into the sack, not caring what else he broke.

"Elric, wait. I want to come with you." Wynn jogged into the clearing, her hair a wild mess tangled with leaves and twigs. She was carrying the two pieces of the spoon in her leaf-covered hat.

"No." He slung his sack over his shoulder, leaving hers lying on the ground. "Do what you want. I don't care. But I don't want to see you again."

He turned his back on her and walked away.

He couldn't do this anymore. He couldn't. It was too much.

And now she had destroyed the one thing that meant anything to him.

He didn't look back over his shoulder. He didn't listen for footsteps behind him. If she wasn't going to obey him, then there was nothing he could do for her. He'd tried.

The light was fading quickly, and he wouldn't be able to keep walking through the darkness. He needed a fire to keep foxes and wolves at bay.

The woodland shadows stretched over him as he sat down in a clearing with a patch of spring bluebells at the base of a hill. Using the butt of the ax, he cleared a space for a fire, and hastily gathered a small pile of sticks.

The fire started quickly, and Elric crouched near the dim and flickering light. Pulling his cloak over his shoulders, he tried to stave off the chill that came with the deepening night.

Wynn would be in the dark.

He let out a huff.

He couldn't do this. It had taken too much from him. Elric closed his eyes and tried to remember the last thing Mother had said to him. Something about making sure to clean the mud from his shoes.

He didn't get to say good-bye. He left thinking they

would have endless days, and a million chances to speak with one another, to say, what?

That he still needed her? That he wasn't ready to be grown up just yet?

Those are things he never would have said to her out loud. Even if they had another day, he would have come into the hut and not noticed the way the lingering scent of thyme and sage hung in the air from the drying herbs in the window. He would have teased his mother about the one or two gray hairs that peppered her braid, not knowing he would never see her with hair silver from age. He would eat whatever she had cooking in her pot, and it would taste like summer herbs and vegetables grown by her hand. Then he would leave the house complaining that he didn't need her to fuss over him even though he felt loved when she did, and she would have said, "I'll see you again soon, my boy."

Elric sniffed, and wiped his nose on the back of his sleeve.

"I'm sorry, Mum," he whispered to himself as he watched the flames dance in the deep shadows.

CHAPTER FIFTEEN
Wynn

WYNN LOOKED UP AT THE gray sky through the dark branches of the oaks. It was getting dark. Elric wasn't coming back. He was angry.

She knew how that felt.

She was still angry too. The strands in the front of her hair wouldn't stay out of her face.

Wynn slapped it back and pulled on Osmund's hat. The leaves in her hair made her head itchy.

She looked at the broken spoon.

It snapped when they were fighting. Bad things

happened when they fought, and she didn't like it. She didn't like being quiet all the time either. Elric never told her he was sorry, and he was stubborn like a goat. Mother told her that if you push a goat, the goat will push back. If you want a goat to follow you, fill your pockets with weeds.

Besides, Osmund told her to take care of her brother, and she promised she would do it, even when he was acting like a goat. She just wished he wouldn't be mean when she helped.

Wynn lifted the spoon and tried to fit the pieces back the way they were. If she turned them and pushed them together just right, they didn't look broken and were only a little crooked. She needed them to stick.

An owl hooted.

"Mildred, come." She stooped and motioned to the chicken. The hen came running to her. Wynn tucked her in the sack. The hen poked her head out and clucked softly in Wynn's ear.

It would be nighttime soon.

She could mend the spoon. At least, she would try, and then Elric could be happy again. She could make this better for him, even though he couldn't mend her hair. She would be good to him anyway, because it was right. Mother liked it when she was kind, and she would have repaired the spoon for him. Wynn was a good sister, no matter what. She needed to find something sticky to hold the spoon together.

Honey was sticky.

Wynn frowned. It made Elric angry when she used all the honey last time.

What else was sticky?

Wynn turned in a slow circle. The only things near her were trees, a lot of trees.

And trees had sap.

Wynn wandered through the darkening shadows as the moon rose on the horizon. The stars began to appear in the dimming twilight, but they didn't look very bright in the light of the moon. Sap was tree blood. It came out of a wound. She needed to find a broken branch.

An owl hooted again. There seemed to be noises everywhere. Each of her footsteps sounded loud in the crunchy leaves. She didn't like the dark, and as she walked, she felt like something was following close behind her waiting to grab her. She thought about the Grendel coming at night to eat people.

She shuddered. She needed to find her brother quickly. She didn't want to be alone in the woods, and she didn't want him to be alone either. At least the moon was big and bright, rising in a deep-blue sky, but a strange shadow was creeping over it.

As Wynn looked at the moon, she noticed a broken branch. It was up high in a tree. She would have to climb it.

"Stay here, Mildred," she whispered to the hen. "There are owls and foxes out." She didn't want to mention the Grendel to the hen as she looped the sack over a short branch of a tree. He was too scary.

Wynn reached as high as she could and grabbed on tight to a low limb. She struggled to pull herself onto the branch. The bark scratched her palms and raked over the bare skin of her calf when her leggings fell back.

The tree shook as she climbed, and Wynn held on tight. Her stomach wobbled as she hesitated. She'd have to reach her leg out over the open air to step up on the next branch.

She trembled as she hugged the trunk of the tree and reached with the tip of her toe.

She felt as if she were falling, even though she still clung to the tree. Finally her toe perched on the branch. She didn't fall down, but now she couldn't move either. If she let go, she would fall.

Mildred clucked, and a breeze rustled the new spring leaves around her. "Elric," she called, but her voice muffled against her shoulder as she held tight to the tree.

She waited, shaking. Somehow her brother would know that she was in trouble. He always did.

But he didn't come.

She had to do this on her own.

Wynn shifted her weight, testing the branch with her toe as she pulled herself next to the broken limb. As she reached, her lower foot came away from the branch and she found herself standing on the toes of one foot. She didn't want to think about that. If she stretched, she could reach the broken place. The thin branch beneath her foot shuddered as she reached inside the wounded tree and felt for the stickiest sap. Wynn scraped half-dried balls of goo with her fingers. The sap pushed under her nails and stuck to her sleeve. Once her hand was coated in it, she looked down.

The ground seemed so far, and now she couldn't use her hand. She didn't want to lose the sap. Shifting her weight again, she scraped the side of her foot along the tree trunk, looking for the lower branch with her toe. The rough bark pressed against her cheek.

She prodded with her toe, but she couldn't see the

branch and she couldn't turn her head to look. Her grip slipped on the trunk and she clawed at the bark. It didn't do any good. She touched the lower branch with her toe, but as she leaned her weight on it, she tipped backward. Her foot slipped, and she dropped, catching the limb under her arm, as her chin slammed down hard against it.

Wynn screamed, dangling from the branch, her legs kicking in the air. "Elric!"

Her heart pounded. It beat so hard it was painful. She couldn't hold on. The branch slipped out of her grip, the bark scraping across her palms. Then there was nothing around her at all but a swooping sensation as she fell.

She landed in a crumpled heap in a pile of leaves. Her mind spun, trying to sort through what happened. Her hands and arms stiffened, then shook so hard she couldn't control them. At first she couldn't breathe in. All the air had left her chest.

Then finally her throat opened enough that she could gasp, and she coughed. Her head ached, and her body hurt all over. Her arm and leg throbbed from hitting the branches and slowing her fall, and her skin burned from her scratches. The muscles in her arm relaxed, and her thoughts finally knew she was on the ground.

She carefully moved her arms and legs. In spite of her fall, she didn't think she broke any bones.

Wynn sat up. Her sappy hand was coated in leaves, and her sleeve had stuck to it. Groaning, she got to her feet and retrieved the spoon.

She used the broken end of the spoon to scrape the sap off her palm, then fit the two pieces together. The edge of her sleeve stuck to it, so she ripped the sticky bit of fabric off and wrapped it around the handle.

There!

The handle had a slight crook in it, but it was one piece again. Wynn waved it around like it was a magic wand.

Elric would be happy. Now she needed to find him. She still didn't like that he was cranky and bossy. She still hated her hair. But he was the only brother she had. Maybe now he would be sorry.

Wynn struggled to her feet. Her knees wobbled as she ignored her aches and pains and lifted her sack off the low branch.

She could smell smoke in the clear night air and shivered. It was cold and a fire would be nice. She couldn't start one on her own without the flint. Wynn looped the sack over her shoulder and started walking as Mildred clucked sleepily.

Elric didn't listen to her. That was the problem. Sometimes he talked to her like she was Mildred. Wynn liked to talk to Mildred, but Mildred was a chicken. She didn't talk back, not really. Wynn wasn't certain if the chicken understood or not, and in the end it didn't matter. She liked Mildred anyway.

That was how being with Elric felt—like even if she said something, it didn't matter to him. She didn't really understand him. He said things to her, and asked her things, but he didn't really want her answer. She had answers. She understood lots of things. He just didn't know it.

Wynn rubbed her chest.

She didn't know very many people. Growing up, she had to stay hidden away, and so she only really knew Mother. Father scared her, and Elric was her only friend.

Or she was his chicken.

She straightened Osmund's hat. Osmund listened to her. He gave her a lot of time to speak and let her form her words without guessing what she was going to say before she could say it. That was nice.

She wished Elric could listen to her the same way.

"I don't want to be alone," Wynn said out loud to hear her words. She knew they didn't sound right, but they were her words.

Mildred let out a soft, trilling coo, as if she understood.

The woods were so quiet. Wynn sang under her breath so she wouldn't feel so alone.

> *"My queen, my queen, show me the way.*
> *The moon held in your hands.*
> *In dark of night, the skies rain stars,*
> *And lead me to your lands.*
> *Please grant to me your silver branch,*
> *And through the gate I'll find you."*

The trees thinned until Wynn came upon an enormous clearing on the swell of a small hill. At the top, an old oak had long ago been split by lightning, and yet it still lived. The branches on either side reached up like the fingers of two enormous hands that had not yet grown their spring leaves.

The full moon seemed to rest in their palms, but the strange shadow covered it completely now, turning it reddish orange. The shadow covered almost all of the brightness, and the stars woke, shining beneath the shrouded moon.

This was it. This was from the song. She had found it. They were on the right path to find the Silver Gate.

She would meet the Fairy Queen, and they could sing together. Maybe then she wouldn't be so sad and her magic would come back.

Wynn twirled and danced around the ancient tree, laughing to the moon. As she stopped, she looked down the opposite side of the hill at a small patch of bluebells.

A fire glowed in the heart of them.

CHAPTER SIXTEEN
Elric

THE BREEZE PICKED UP, AND Elric hunched over. It was dark, even though the full moon had risen. That was strange. He looked up; the moon was shrouded in shadow, turning it into a rare blood moon. The warmth from his little fire spread into his hands and face, but did little for the rest of his body. Or the ill feeling in the pit of his stomach. Wynn was probably huddled in the grove where he left her, curled under her cloak, alone and afraid. He'd have to go back for her. He couldn't leave her alone all night.

It didn't matter how angry he was at her. She was his only sister, and he missed her. No matter how miserable things got, she was always happy, and he didn't realize how much he needed that sometimes. He didn't like to see her upset.

And it was his fault.

Footsteps clambered down the hill behind him. He whipped around just in time to have Wynn crash into his chest. They both tumbled into the bluebells.

"Elric!" she squealed. "Hurry, hurry!"

"Careful, the fire is right there." He pushed her off him and struggled to his feet. She bounced up and offered him a hand. At least he didn't have to go searching for her again, though she was a mess, with leaves and twigs stuck all over her.

"Come look," she said, her eyes large, and expression urgent. She grabbed his hand and pulled with all her strength until he followed.

The top of the hill was crowned with an old tree that had been split by lightning sometime when it still was young. Now it had grown in two halves.

"It's a tree," he said to her.

"No, look here." She tugged him around to the far side of the hill, and from where they stood, the blood moon looked like it was balanced in the branches of the tree. "Like the song," she said.

It took a minute for Elric to realize what she was talking about. He had to sing her song in his head until he came to the verse about the Fairy Queen holding the moon. The branches of the old tree did resemble hands. But the song was just a song.

"It's very pretty, but it can't be from the song. The song doesn't say anything about a tree, and the stars aren't about to rain down on us." Elric took a step back toward his little fire, but Wynn grabbed him again.

"Look!" she insisted, pointing at the sky.

Elric gazed up, and in the deep indigo of the night sky, tiny streaks of light fell through the darkness before disappearing back into it. The stars around them floated in a pale and distant cloud of light, washed by the shaded moonlight, but no less amazing in its beauty.

In his life, Elric had never seen anything like it. He rarely looked at the stars. At night he kept his attention focused on the edges of dark thickets that hid dangerous wild creatures, or on his flock. If he did look skyward, it always seemed to be clouded and gray. As he watched the night sky, hundreds of falling stars flashed through the darkness like tiny drops of rain.

Overcome, Elric sat. He couldn't say anything. He watched the falling stars, trying to take in the whole sky at once. In every moment when the sky remained still, he anticipated a new flash of light. When it came, he still was surprised by it.

Wynn crossed her legs and plopped down next to him. She swung her sack off her shoulder and let Mildred struggle out. The hen jumped onto Elric's lap and nestled down there, fluffing her soft feathers. Elric stroked her wings, glad that they were friends again, and she'd stopped trying to peck him. In that moment it was as if the three of them were a small piece of something vast and magical. Peace settled over the night. The shadow slowly left the moon, and Elric felt fate as if it were a thing he could touch hanging in the starlit sky.

"Will we find the gate?" Wynn asked.

Elric couldn't tear his gaze from the stars above. "I don't know," he admitted. Osmund's words passed through is mind. *What matters is what you believe.*

The Silver Gate was nothing but a fairy tale, but when he saw something as wondrous as this, the boy in him—the one who still loved to hear his mother's stories and imagined a life of glory and adventure—wondered.

Wynn held something out to him. "I made it better."

He glanced down at the spoon in her hand.

His chest tightened as he reached out and took it from her. Sap stuck to his fingers as he touched the awkward bandage she had patched together. He looked at his sister in the brightening moonlight and saw the dirt and leaves clinging to her. She must have been covered in sap. A scrape marred her cheek. "What did you do?"

"I climbed up a tree. Then I fell down." She picked at the sap clinging to her palm and pulled off her hat to scratch her head.

"Wynn!" How in the world did she get herself up a tree? "Are you hurt? Why would you do such a thing?" He reached over and pulled one of the leaves from her hair.

"It is Mother's spoon, and you were sad, so I found sap to mend it." She let out a heavy sigh. "I'm sorry I broke it."

A twinge of guilt gnawed at him. "You weren't the only one who broke it. But thank you for mending it. Mother used to let me play with it while she was cooking. When I hold it, it feels like she's not really gone."

"Mother brushed my hair every night." Wynn paused, and her eyebrows came together as if she were concentrating really hard on something. Elric waited for her words. They took a long time to come. He wanted to say something, anything, to prompt her to speak, but he had no idea what she was going to say, and her silence stretched until it became uncomfortable. "I felt—"

"Like she cared for you," he finished.

She glared at him. "No. Listen."

Elric leaned back, stunned. Both words came out so clear that they didn't sound like her. They sounded like the girl she would have been, the one who had been stolen as a baby.

A silence fell over them again. Elric waited for her words to come again.

"I felt . . ." Her gaze dropped and her hands pulled into fists. "Normal."

It was Elric's turn not to speak. He didn't know what to say. Guilt ate at him as ferociously as the Grendel. He'd hurt her. He'd really hurt her, and he'd taken something precious away from her without understanding what it meant to her. It was wrong. A deep sadness tightened around his heart.

He turned the spoon over in his hands. The tacky sap clung to his fingers. "I'm sorry," he finally said. "I shouldn't have cut your hair, and I hurt you. I haven't been a very good brother." He'd been acting more like a shepherd with her, pushing her around, even shearing her. He drew the severed braid from his belt. "I promise I'll do better."

She touched it, and the sap on her fingers stuck to the fine hairs. She carefully tucked it in her belt, the way he carried his spoon. He placed an arm over her shoulders.

"Thank you," she said, her eyes glassy in the dim light.

He stood, and Mildred hopped to the ground, flipping her wings with an irritated flick. He reached out a hand to his sister, and she took it, the sap sealing their palms together. The shadow passed the moon, and the full brightness of the moon's face revealed itself as the shadow slowly waned. The stars dimmed, and it became harder and harder to see the ones that fell.

Together they walked to the fire. For the rest of the night, Elric made up a story of a brave knight and a fearsome dragon off on adventures together while he carefully pulled the leaves and twigs out of Wynn's hair and combed it until all the tangles came free.

The next morning, the sun shone brightly in a clear blue sky. The sound of Wynn singing greeted Elric upon waking, and he smiled. He picked up an acorn and flicked it at her. It hit her on the shoulder and she spun around. She picked up a fairly hefty oak branch and pointed it at him like a sword.

The curly wood wouldn't make a very useful weapon, but that didn't matter to his sister. Elric searched the ground for another acorn and tossed it at her. She swung the branch and managed to knock the acorn in a different direction.

Wynn jumped up and down in delight and fell into a laughter that came from every part of her body at once in gasping, hiccuping bursts. He had been making her laugh like that his whole life. He didn't realize how much he had missed it. It was good to have his Wynn back. He was determined not to chase her away ever again.

"Get this one," he said, and flung another acorn at her. She swung, but missed, spinning around entirely. Elric laughed too. He couldn't remember the last time he'd done something simply for fun.

"You do it." Wynn handed him the branch. He used it to push himself to his feet.

She picked up an acorn and threw it at him, but she flung it straight at the ground between them. Mildred chased after it and pecked it. She grabbed the acorn in her beak and trotted away with it. Wynn giggled as she watched the hen run. "Try again," he said, stepping forward.

Wynn picked up another and threw it better this time. He swung the branch as hard as he could, but missed the nut completely.

A red squirrel chattered at him from a tree, and Wynn giggled. Elric smiled. "You're pretty good."

She beamed and crossed her arms. "I *am* good."

Elric chased her down to ruffle her hair. The sun rose high on the horizon, so they packed up their things and threw dust on the fire. It didn't take long to hike up the hill until they stood beneath the enormous branches of the split oak.

In the light of day, the magic had left it. It was just an old tree.

"Where do we go?" Wynn asked, feeding Mildred some new spring grass.

"We'll keep heading north. The farther we get from the village, the safer we'll be." Elric looked at the vast wilderness stretching out before them.

"How will we cross the clouds?" Wynn asked.

"What are you talking about?" Elric shouldered his sack and set off.

Wynn caught up to him and let Mildred down on the

ground. "The song. We found hands holding the moon. Now we have to cross the clouds."

To prove her point she sang until she came to the verse,

> *"My queen, my queen, I'll follow true,*
> *The path so hard to find.*
> *Across the clouds, a lake of air,*
> *Will lead me to your kind.*
> *Please grant to me your silver branch,*
> *And through the gate I'll find you."*

"Wynn, there were no hands. It was only a tree, and the next verse is impossible," Elric said. "You can't cross the clouds, and lakes aren't made of air."

"We found the hands and the stars," Wynn insisted. "We *will* find the lake."

Elric didn't argue. He was looking for a village, a hamlet, or even a friendly recluse who could use an extra hand or two. He would have to hide Wynn away from others, the way Mother had done. He'd have to build her a hut deep in the woods somewhere, then come to check on her as often as his work allowed. They would find a way to survive. They had to. And once they were settled into a new life, Wynn would forget about their quest and they could move on.

Wynn picked up a stick from the old split oak and whacked the ground with it. "When we find the Silver Gate, you will believe me."

"Sure, Wynn." Elric took the oak branch and turned it over into a walking stick. "We'll find it." He could let her have her fantasies. He just wouldn't count on them himself.

CHAPTER SEVENTEEN

Elric

THE PATH NORTH BECAME EASIER, though they traveled for days without any sign of another village. Elric tried his hand at trapping food with Osmund's snare, but too few small animals had come out of their winter sleep, water birds had not yet returned north, and the plants were only beginning to bud.

Their supply of food was growing thin.

The path began to climb as they came near the fells, great hills, and mountains that rose on either side of deep valleys and canyons. The sun had risen, but Elric couldn't see it. A heavy dampness hung in the air. His stomach rumbled, but he ignored the pangs of hunger. He hadn't eaten at all the day before, but Wynn hadn't noticed. He didn't want her to. Every night, he set the snare, and every morning he found it empty.

Wynn dragged her stick along the ground as the plants beneath their feet crunched under the still-dead ravages of the recent winter. "I'm hungry," she said. "I want some cheese. I like cheese."

"The cheese is gone." Elric leaned on his own stick as he searched for a path up a steep hill. "So is the bread." A narrow rut wove back and forth across the incline. They'd have to walk five times the distance to climb to the top of the ridge.

"What can we eat?" she asked.

Elric's stomach cramped as he slid his sack off his shoulder. They had packed extra cloth and tinder in Wynn's sack with a layer of dried grasses and moss for Mildred to nest on. He'd kept the food with him, just in case. Elric reached in the sack and found the last leathery bit of dried meat. Wynn didn't like dried meat. She had a hard time chewing it, but it was all they had left.

"Here, have this," he said, handing it to her.

She frowned, but took a bite without complaining.

She must have been hungry. Wynn squinted through the blanketing mists at the trail ahead. Elric sighed as his stomach rumbled again. This time Wynn must have heard it, because she stopped. Without a word, she handed him the rest of the meat.

"You eat it," he insisted. He could withstand a little hunger.

"No." She waved it at him, and he took it from her hand.

He took a small bite, when he really wanted to rip half the chunk off with his teeth and gnaw on it until the cramping pain in his stomach ceased. But he knew the hunger would not end, so he handed the rest back to her.

Elric watched the last of their food disappear, and the gray fog around them seemed all the more bleak. He felt the strain in his thighs and shins as he leaned on his oak stick to climb up the mountain. Wynn slowed down, still chewing on the last bit of dried meat.

In the distance, they heard a clattering of pots. Elric held out his hand, and Wynn tucked herself behind him, now wary of strangers.

A swarthy, wizened-looking old man clattered down the road with a load of old tools hanging off his back.

Elric stayed very still, keeping his hand on the handle of Osmund's ax.

"Hello there?" Elric called out.

The old man didn't answer. Elric gripped the ax tighter.

When the man finally reached them, he looked up through clouded eyes and blinked at them. "Does this road lead south?" he asked.

Elric glanced behind him, wondering if they could really call the path they were on a road. "Yes, at the bottom of the hill," he said.

"Ah." The old man nodded sagely, his tongue poking out through a gap in his teeth. "Do you have pots to trade?"

"No," Elric answered. They had only one pot, and he wasn't willing to give it up.

"Very well, have a good day." The man wheezed as he waddled past them.

Wynn gripped Elric's elbow, her eyes wide.

"Excuse me!" Elric called. It took the old man several moments to turn around, and Elric could swear he heard the peddler's bones creak as he did so. "Is there a village nearby?"

"Hmm." He turned back. "There is a village on the

edge of the lake. I haven't been there since the summer. They are fishermen. Wanted to trade for hooks and nets. I don't need hooks and nets. Only pots." He coughed out a laugh, then turned back around and started down the hill, and the clattering of his pots faded to silence.

Elric's heart felt lighter than it had for months. He turned to Wynn. "Did you hear that? There's a village nearby! At the top of the hill, we should be able to see the lake he talked about. We'll have a home soon, and fresh fish for dinner." His mouth watered at the prospect of a hot meal.

"I like fish," Wynn said. "But not as much as cheese."

Elric chuckled and gave Wynn a friendly push with his elbow.

"What do you think the Fairy Queen will be like?" she asked as they continued their hike.

"I don't know," Elric said. He focused on putting one foot in front of the next as he trudged up the hill. The trail turned steep, and they had to turn a sharp corner to track back up the mountain the way they had come. Back and forth, back and forth, they wound their way along the path.

Elric used his walking stick to brace himself as he gave Wynn a hand. Mildred had to flap her wings, but eventually she made it onto the path.

"Is she pretty?" Wynn tried again.

These sorts of questions served no purpose, and Wynn was full of them at times. But sometimes the only way to stop them from coming was to answer them, and he was more in the mood to humor her now that they had a goal. They would make it to the village soon.

He remembered the dream he'd had, and a vision swirling with the memory of heavily falling snow. "The Fairy Queen is very pretty." The soft earth of the trail crumbled beneath one of his feet, slipping downhill. Elric took greater care placing his next step and held a hand for Wynn so she wouldn't fall.

"What does she look like?" Wynn asked, teetering as she walked along the narrow path.

"Magical and very regal. She has dark brown skin and white hair that floats around her instead of falling to her shoulders," Elric began. Another switchback in the trail forced him to help Wynn up the path and let her lead. He found himself leaning toward the uphill slope even though the mist hid the height that they had climbed.

"Really?" Wynn asked between pants. Her chest heaved with her breaths, and Elric worried that the climb might be too much for her.

He kept talking to keep her distracted. "It's true. She has eyes that glow with different colors, sometimes blue like the sky, and sometimes gold like the fields of summer. But beware if they are red, for it means she is angry and determined to cause trouble."

Wynn laughed, but it made her breath seem even more labored. The mist was thinner here. They had to be near the top. "She wears a dress of woven spiderwebs and dew, decorated with flowers and vines that grow up over her body." Again, the memory of a world of winter white filled his mind. "Or sometimes in winter, her dress is made of frost and ice. It shimmers in the light, pure as snow."

"Pretty," Wynn said wistfully as her fingers slid over the frayed hem of her mutilated dress. They rested on the severed braid tucked into her belt. "Is she kind?"

What was Elric supposed to say to that? Every tale he had ever heard about the Fairy Queen said that she stole healthy children to keep as her own, and left . . .

He looked at his sister. She smiled brightly, her expression full of innocence and hope. He didn't want to even think the word that their father had so often placed upon her.

A monster.

That wasn't true. Wynn was the furthest thing from a monster that he had ever known.

Wynn didn't seem disturbed by his silence. "I think the Fairy Queen is kind," she said as the sun brightened the path ahead. She trotted forward, then climbed up an outcropping of rocks.

Elric sprinted to get beneath her to catch her should she fall. Instead she rose triumphantly on the crest of rocks and placed her hands on her hips like a conquering knight. "Oh, look!"

Elric found a handhold and tested a thin stone ledge with his toe before he scrambled up the rock and pulled himself beside her.

The morning sun shone brightly in the blue sky above them. As they looked down, the valleys were filled with thick mist. The fog stretched out before them like a blanket of the purest lamb's wool, until it seemed as if they stood on an island of rock floating on an ocean of clouds.

Elric had never been so high above the world and wondered if this is what it was like to be a bird that soared beyond the gray that covered all of the world he knew.

Still, it was strange to see a thick blanket of fog at this time of the year. Patches of snow still clung to the ground. Usually mists followed the cool nights of the harvest, not the first warm rains of spring.

"It's beautiful," Wynn whispered. She drew her cloak around her shoulders and hugged herself. "Cross the clouds."

"Huh?" Mildred flapped near his foot, and he lifted her so she could perch on his shoulder. Her soft feathers tickled his ear.

"The song. We cross the clouds." Wynn pointed across the fell. A large peak rose up, still covered in spring snow. "To the white mountain."

"Wynn." Her name came out as an exasperated plea. "We have bigger problems to worry about than the song. We can't see the lake with the fog in the valleys."

The last thing they needed was to get lost in the fells.

Wynn seemed undeterred. She climbed down on the opposite side of the crag and started marching down the hill.

"Wait," Elric called, tucking Mildred in the crook of his arm and hopping down rock to rock. The soil seemed looser on this side of the hill. Footing was tricky.

"We're almost there." Wynn didn't heed the soil

sliding out from each fall of her foot as it created heavy footprints in the new spring grass. "We will find the lake."

Elric's heart raced as he took long strides to catch up to her, but he had to place his feet carefully and couldn't move quickly enough to reach her. "Slow down!"

"Hurry," she called back. She took a bold step forward onto a mound of smooth dirt at the edge of a muddy runoff ditch created by recent rain. There was no grass there to hold the earth stable.

"Wynn, don't!" he called, but it was too late. The earth crumbled beneath her.

CHAPTER EIGHTEEN
Elric

"WYNN!" ELRIC DROPPED MILDRED AND jumped forward down the slope. He threw his feet in front of him so he could slide on his hip over the slick grass. Soft ground churned under his heel as he dug it into the earth to slow his descent.

"Help!" Wynn screamed from somewhere below him.

"I'm coming!" He slid faster down the hill, trying to follow the runoff ditch she had fallen into. Finally he saw her through the fog—at least, he saw her hands, and the top of her head clinging to an exposed rock on the edge of a drop-off.

Elric immediately flipped over onto his stomach and grasped for the grasses and weeds. They slipped so quickly through his hands, the stalks and thorns sliced through his fingers like knives. He kicked his feet and knees into the earth until he slowed to a stop as his foot pushed off the edge of the outcropping and hung over nothingness. Sweat dripped over his face as his heart thrummed in his chest.

"Hold on." Elric crawled over to Wynn and flattened himself on the wet grasses and weeds. He reached out and grasped her wrist with one hand. He tried to lift her up, but he almost pulled himself down with her. He needed something to grasp on to. Reaching over his shoulder, he tugged at the ax, but it was tied too tightly to his sack.

"I fall!" Wynn cried. Mud and tears streaked down her face, and blood poured out of her cut lip.

"I won't let you." He squeezed her wrist tighter. "Don't you let go."

Elric pulled as hard as he could, and the ax came free. He didn't have much leverage lying on his stomach, but he managed to swing the handle with enough force to anchor the blade in the soft earth. "I've got you." He gripped the ax handle as tight as he could and pulled on her wrist.

Wynn pressed her lips together, blood streaking down her chin. With a determined look in her eye, she gripped his arm with her other hand.

"Pull," Elric grunted as he strained to drag her back up onto the bank.

His grip on the ax slipped, and Wynn let out a terrified squeal. Elric heaved with all his might, dragging his sister back to safety. Her upper body landed on the grass next to him, and she threw her leg up. He grabbed her knee and pulled her the rest of the way.

Wynn scrambled next to him and clung to his tunic as he wrapped an arm around her and helped her up the slope away from the ledge. He could feel her shaking and crying against his shoulder, and all he could do was fall back against the cold ground and hold on to her.

"You're safe." His voice came out choked and uneven, and his arms felt as if they had lost all their bones. "I've got you."

They rested on the grassy slope long enough for the sun to rise over the fells and burn away some of the mist. Mildred chortled happily as she stalked through the weeds, looking for bugs. When she reached the drop off, she hopped up on the rock that Wynn had been clinging to. With her head cocked to the side, she peered over the edge, and let out a low and cautious *awwwk*. Then she crept away from the edge with her head low and her wings hunched.

Even the hen knew a dangerous drop when she saw one. Elric pushed himself up and checked Wynn's arms and legs for scrapes. "Are you hurt?" His muscles ached, and his hip felt bruised, but he didn't think anything was broken.

She touched her lip, and her hand came away smeared with blood. She stared at it, but didn't say anything.

"Here." Elric pulled his sack over, glad that for the first time that it was mostly empty. Very little fell out when they slid down the hill. He found the small jar of honey. It was a miracle it hadn't broken. Scooping his finger around the rim, he dabbed some on Wynn's lip.

She tasted it and smiled, in spite of the fact the color hadn't quite returned to her face.

With the mists in retreat, Elric took a peek at the ridge they had nearly gone over. He whistled low under his breath.

The drop-off made him dizzy as he helped Wynn up.

"Whatever you do, don't look down," he said. They'd have to walk along the edge of it, until they could find a safe path down into the valley. "And next time you decide to fall off a mountain, learn to fly first."

Wynn giggled nervously, but her hands still shook as she followed precisely in his footsteps, limping as she walked. She held on to his arm the entire way down. Mildred stayed far from the treacherous edge, still cooing in low and cautious tones. Once they reached the valley floor, Elric felt as if he had entered a strange and different world.

The air turned cool and hazy. It touched his skin, then lingered there, making him feel as if they were being watched, even though the valley was still. He remembered Osmund's words, about how the presence of the Grendel felt like oil on his skin, and he hastily wiped his face. The ominous feeling wouldn't leave him.

"It's quiet," Wynn said, her voice hushed as if the stillness itself had somehow seeped into her. The rocks lay scattered about at the bottom of the hills, jagged and haphazard obstacles in their path, a reminder that at any moment another one could come rolling off one of the fells. It would be impossible to set a snare to catch food here, and even more difficult to find their way across.

"Don't worry," Elric said as he adjusted the pack on his shoulder so the ax lay flat against his back. "Once the mist burns off, the birds will come out. And in the better light, we're sure to find a road. We'll be to the village soon."

Wynn took his hand and stayed close to his side. He didn't say the truth that tumbled through his mind. They would find no roads here. No one in their right mind would choose to travel through this place. They were lost.

Even with the sun high, the mist lingered, isolating them in a lonely fog as they wandered through the fells.

Elric couldn't tell how long they had been walking. Wynn hobbled along next to him as they climbed through the rocks of the bottom of a ravine. His head ached but not more than his stomach. Every time he had to lift his arms to haul himself over another stone, his body felt as if it were being pulled to the ground with heavy weights.

Wynn's steps came slowly, and she had grown too quiet, staring at the ground, her eyes drooping sleepily.

"I'm hungry," she mumbled as she pressed her arm across her middle.

Elric looked around. There was nothing but mist, rocks, grassy ledges up steep hillsides, and pools of stagnant water buzzing with insects. A dead tree clung to the side of the hill, reaching across the ravine as if it could find hope on the other side. A tiny rivulet fell over the rocks, splashing water onto moss-covered stones before it disappeared into the gravel.

"Let's sit. We can rest." He fell onto a rock, his stomach cramped. He hadn't eaten more than a tiny bite of dried meat in days. It had taken so much out of him to climb the mountain, and he used up whatever energy he had left when Wynn fell.

"You are worried," Wynn said as she pulled her sack around and laid it in her lap.

"I have a good reason to be," Elric admitted. "We have nothing left. The village could be days away yet, if we find it at all."

Mildred poked her head out of Wynn's sack and clucked sleepily. It must be nice for her. She was growing fat on bugs and spring grubs.

"Don't worry." Wynn placed her hand on his and gave it a pat, but her words offered him little comfort. He couldn't *not* worry.

"Come on, Wynn. We have to keep going," he said. Sitting on a rock wasn't going to help their situation, but finding the village would. He put an arm over her shoulder and tried to think like her. She never worried about anything. She lived in the moment.

That moment he was hungry. His stomach let out an angry growl.

"You are hungry," Wynn said, even as her own stomach answered his. "You have to eat." Her brow wrinkled as her smile turned down into a thoughtful frown. She swung the sack off her shoulder and clung to it.

"What are we going to eat? Rocks?" he asked. "I don't think they'd be very good for our teeth."

She let out a chuckle. "Rocks don't taste very good."

"I don't want to know how you know that," he said. He pushed himself up from the boulder slowly, gathering a dried limb that had fallen from the dead tree. He needed to make a fire, but he didn't feel like he had much strength left. The ax swung slowly, and his fingers stumbled with the flint. He dropped the striking stone, failing to catch it again as it fell.

Wynn picked it up and handed it to him. "We will find food."

"How?" He took the flint and let the sharp edge of it dig into his palm. "We can't just wish for food and have it magically appear in our sack."

Wynn scrunched up her face and closed her eyes

tight. She balled her hands into fists and then began to shake.

"Wynn, what are you doing?" Elric fought the urge to laugh. "You look ridiculous."

"I'm wishing," she said between her gritted teeth.

"Wishing?" Now he did laugh. It looked like she was trying to lay an egg. "I didn't think wishing took that much effort."

"I'm wishing hard." She opened her eyes and glared at him, before twisting her face up again.

"That's not going to work," he said. "You should stop before you hurt yourself. Wishes aren't real. They don't actually come true."

This time she peeked one eye open and gave him a skeptical look. "Wishes come true."

"I've never had a wish come true." He arranged the bits of dried branch into a pile that would catch fire quickly. Wynn pulled Mildred out of the sack and set the hen in her lap.

"Have you *ever* wished?" Wynn asked, stroking the hen.

Elric opened his mouth to say something, but then hesitated. *Had* he ever made a wish? If he did, he couldn't recall it.

She gave him a small smile as she reached into the empty sack for some of Mildred's dried grass. They had been using it as tinder every night. Suddenly she let out a squeal.

"What?" Elric jumped at the sudden noise. "What is it?"

"Look." Wynn held out her hand, and there, cradled in her palm, was a single perfect egg.

CHAPTER NINETEEN
Elric

"MILDRED, I COULD KISS YOU!" Elric called, scooping the hen off of Wynn's lap and swinging her around. She flapped her wings and squawked as Elric kissed the top of her head. The chicken wriggled out of his hands and trotted off, as if she were deeply offended. "Let me see that," he said as he took the egg from his sister and carried it back to the small trickle of water. "I'll start the fire. You gather the sticks?"

Wynn nodded and followed after the hen.

Elric cradled the precious egg in his palms. Something

warm blossomed in his chest, and for a moment he forgot about his hunger. He held hope.

He filled the little pot with water from the tiny stream and then carefully placed the egg inside. It looked so small, and it wouldn't be enough to fill either of their bellies, but it was something.

His hands shook as he started the fire, but it didn't take long for the tinder to catch. He broke off some smaller branches of the dead tree and fed the tiny flames. The sky had grown red, and it would be dark in the ravine soon with the shadows of the high hills over them.

"Millie-lee-lee-lee!" he shouted, trilling the last syllable until it echoed against the hills.

Mildred fluttered over a large rock and came to him, exactly as he'd taught her. Elric walked over to her and the hen hopped onto his shoulder. He stroked the soft feathers of her breast. "Good girl," he cooed. She pecked his ear.

It seemed he was forgiven for ruffling her feathers.

Elric sat on a rock and watched the egg in the pot while Mildred hunted for crickets between the rocks. It took forever for the water to boil.

Once the water was roiling, Elric looked around to see if Wynn was near. She walked slowly up the path with something bundled in the edge of her ripped skirt.

Elric trotted over to help her with whatever she was carrying. "Where are the sticks?" he asked.

"Look what I have." She held out her improvised basket. It was teeming with soft-looking leaves in the shape of the foot of a goose. "It's fat hen." Her eyes were bright as she looked up at him.

"Isn't that a weed?" He knew the sheep liked to eat it.

"We can cook it. Mother did." She pushed the pile of soft leaves to the side. "I found this."

"Mushrooms!" A bunch of them. "These are the good ones." He threw an arm around her shoulders and led her over to the fire.

The egg danced merrily in the boiling pot. He sat next to Wynn, who scooped up Mildred and fed her some of the leaves.

When the egg was ready, he stirred the bounty of leaves and mushrooms until they were soft and steaming.

It was a feast.

The soft egg tasted creamy in Elric's mouth. It may have been only two bites, but it filled him with warmth. And the fat hen didn't taste half bad with the earthy mushrooms.

Their own *fat hen* liked it as well. She clucked in contentment as she closed her eyes and tucked her beak into the feathers of her chest.

Elric stroked her. "I'm glad Mildred is with us," he said. And to think he had ordered Wynn to send the hen back home.

"I'm happy." Wynn patted the bird's back. "Mildred is my friend."

She was a part of their little family, and Elric couldn't imagine the journey without her. Mildred opened one eye to peer at him, then closed it again. He knew it wasn't possible, but the bird seemed to be smiling.

Wynn leaned close to his side. She sighed sleepily. Elric reached over to tuck her cloak across her body so she would stay warm. Then he recited her favorite story, one he had told her at least five hundred times about a lost princess. Once more didn't feel like a burden.

"I am the princess," she announced, yawning.

"I thought you wanted to be Wynn the Dragon," he teased.

"No, today a princess," she murmured, then she fell to sleep, softly snoring with her head resting against his shoulder.

Mildred climbed into his lap and settled down,

fluffing her feathers. He tucked his cloak around them and watched the fire, very glad he had them both.

Whatever comfort the "feast" had given them faded quickly as they woke to a cold fire and a misting rain. Elric packed up their small camp quickly and gently tucked Mildred into Wynn's sack with a fresh layer of grass beneath her. Hopefully she would lay another egg, but one egg a day wouldn't be enough.

They needed to find shelter, and quickly.

The fells were unforgiving.

Elric led them out of the ravine and into a more open landscape, but the rain came down harder, soaking through their cloaks and thin shoes. Wynn's lips turned blue on the edges, and Elric could see her shaking, though she didn't complain.

In the distance, a steep mountain rose from the narrow valley. Halfway up, Elric could make out the dark streaks of exposed rock forming craggy cliffs.

"We have to make it to that hill." Elric took Wynn's arm so he could support her as they trudged forward through the slanting rain. "We'll look for an outcropping or a cave to stay in until the storm passes. Then maybe we will be able to see the smoke from the village when the weather clears."

They hurried as fast as they could through the valley, but had to cross a narrow stream swollen with cold rain. Elric took three steps out on dry stones, but the stream was too wide to jump. Wynn looked worried on the bank. He held back his hand and helped her out on the rocks, then plunged his foot in.

The icy stream hit him like a punch that nearly knocked the wind out of him. The cold seeped through his muscles and skin with a chilling ache. He stumbled into the current, the water soaking his thighs.

"Mind your feet," Elric warned. The current pulled at Elric's shoe as he braced to help his sister. Wynn jumped into the water, falling so her arm and chest splashed into the deep part of the stream. He pulled her up, but not before she had soaked herself. Together they struggled over the rocky stream bottom to the other side.

They managed to drag themselves up the bank and head to the foot of the steep hill, but it was a long steep climb toward the rocks.

Wynn coughed as Elric tried to support her, keeping her close to his body so he could share what little warmth he had with her. She never gave up, putting one foot in front of another as her wet clothing clung to her body and the relentless storm washed her pale face in cold rain.

"Don't worry, Wynn, we're almost there." Up ahead, he could see a dark shadow beneath the rock. "There's a cave."

"So cold," Wynn whispered.

"We'll start a fire. Just a little farther. We have to keep going." Elric pulled her up a muddy slope, and she clung to a rock, climbing on her own until they reached the mouth of a wide cave. Elric helped Wynn beneath the sheltering rock, and she curled into a small ball, her clothing dripping on the ground. Her whole body trembled, and her teeth clattered.

Elric looked around. The cave wasn't deep, merely the underside of a large outcropping, but it was reasonably protected from the wind and rain. He had to find wood, and something, anything, they could eat. He took his ax and set back out into the rain.

The rain splattered on his back and shoulders. He barely noticed at all—it was more of a creeping cold that sank through his body to his bones. His hunger ate away at his strength as he followed the path down to a cluster of trees on the skirt of the hill.

In the shelter of the grove, he noticed a stump hewn

by an ax. His heart thundered to life at the sign of civilization. They had to be near the village the old man had spoken of.

"Hello!" Elric called into the rain. "Does anyone live here?"

There was no answer. Elric wandered deeper into the grove, where he found a drying shed filled with wood that someone had chopped. It was gray with age and cracked, perfect for starting a fire quickly.

He stacked as many chunks of wood as he could in his arms, and a cluster of sticks.

The way back up to the cave had somehow become steeper, and he wasn't able to use his arms to balance. A raven perched near the trunk of one of the trees. Water dripped from its beak and its feathers rose up in wet spikes. It peered at him and let out a low and ominous caw.

Elric hurried as fast as he could. Twice he lost hold of the logs, spilling them onto the narrow path. He had to take them up again, balancing them until he reached the cave. Wynn stood, but stumbled as she came toward him to help.

"I'll start the fire, but I need you to tend it while I look for something to eat." They would need something more filling than a patch of weeds and a handful of mushrooms. "I think the village is nearby. No matter what, don't let this flame go out."

What he wouldn't give for bread. Elric bent and arranged the sticks, but it took him several tries to light the damp tinder. Eventually he had a small fire glowing. Wynn lifted one of the cut pieces of wood and placed it on the fire, propped up by a rock so the new flame didn't get smothered. "Hurry back," she said, huddling close to the tiny fire.

Elric returned to the grove where he had found the shed and called out louder, "Is anyone out there?" Someone must have cut the wood. He searched the horizon for a hovel, or any sort of house, but found none.

The air smelled cold, like damp earth and grass. No smoke from warm hearths lingered in the air. "Anyone?" he called again, desperate.

A weak bleating answered him.

Elric ran toward the sound, his feet flying over the ground like the swift paws of a wolf.

In a clearing, a newborn lamb lay in the wet grass, its fleece a pure and startling white even in the dreary rain. It struggled to stand, then flopped back on its side, panting with the effort.

Elric turned in a slow circle. There had to be a shepherd nearby. No one left a flock while the ewes dropped their lambs. Any number of things could kill both mother and baby.

Where was the mother?

Elric trotted around the clearing, looking for the lost ewe. The tiny lamb continued to bleat, but did not stand. He saw no sign of the shepherd or the flock. No prints in the mud, nothing.

Where was the shepherd?

Elric's heart pounded.

Someone should be here. Elric knew what it took to protect a flock. It was his duty. He watched over every ewe in his care. He helped every lamb carefully into the world, then nurtured them because one lamb could mean the difference between producing what they owed, or failing to meet their burdens.

He never wanted to be the one who let down the village. They all trusted him with the animals.

Elric bent down and stroked his hand over the lamb's damp face. It kicked and struggled to find its feet, pushing its little head into his palm. It was no use. The poor thing flopped back on its side. It had no mother. It would not survive the night.

He knew the right thing to do. He should put the lamb on his shoulders and search for the village. It had to be close. A heavy wave of rain swept across the clearing.

He couldn't leave Wynn. His middle cramped, nearly doubling him over. They were starving. He could take the lamb back to the cave.

No. He was no thief. Someone else's livelihood was at stake. Another serf owed this lamb to his lord and master. What right did he have to steal it?

But it lay here abandoned, and it would soon die in the rain. Killing it quickly would be merciful.

While that might be true, he knew every beast in his own flock. He would know if one of his lambs disappeared without a trace.

Elric looked at the weakening lamb. No, best to leave the poor thing and let its master find the carcass in the morning.

Elric's stomach growled at him, twisting in pain.

Wynn needed him.

The lamb blinked its dark and innocent eyes. It stopped struggling and lay in the grass like a sacrifice.

Elric drew his knife.

CHAPTER TWENTY
Wynn

WYNN WATCHED THE FLAMES FLICKER over the log. The light was nice, but she was still so cold. She shivered; her stomach growled. She had promised Elric she would tend the fire, and she would do a good job.

Mildred stood next to the flames and preened her damp feathers. Wynn wished she could hold her, because Mildred was warm, but Mildred didn't want to be held. Wynn was too wet.

The rain came down harder. Elric was out there. Wynn hoped he would find food. Maybe if he wished hard enough?

Wynn placed another chunk of wood on the fire, and she listened to the water on the log hiss as the flames touched it. The wind howled through the cave and Wynn let out a startled cry. It sounded like the call of a fearsome beast. Maybe it was the Grendel. Another gust of wind blew through the cave, and the flames went out.

No! Wynn fell to her knees in front of the fire and desperately blew on the glowing embers. She fed them little sticks and puffed until another tiny flame burst to life and climbed up the stick. She had to protect it.

Elric would be back soon, and the fire needed to be hot for him. She had to be helpful.

Wynn moved rocks to make a wall around the flames, to keep them safe from the wind, then used her hat to fan them until larger pieces of wood caught fire.

But the wind kept trying to defeat her. She heard it howl and rage, but she stood between the fury of the storm and her little flames. The fearsome wind sent sprays of cold rain through the mouth of the cave, and as the fire grew, so did the shadows all around her. They climbed up the wall until Wynn could swear she saw a tall, dark form moving within them.

Wynn screamed as she hunched down, covering

her ears with her hands and closing her eyes. It was the Grendel. He was here!

The wind howled again, and the cold rain washed over the back of her neck. Her little fire sputtered.

She needed help. But Elric was gone. Wynn thought she heard a low, rumbling voice laughing like thunder, and she did not dare to open her eyes.

Instead she sang.

> *"My queen, my queen, I'll travel far,*
> *To seek your favor high,*
> *Please grant to me your silver branch,*
> *And through the gate I'll find you."*

The wind screamed in fury, and another rumble of thunder rolled overhead. Wynn repeated the words, over and over, opening her eyes just enough to make sure her little fire was still alive. As she sang, the light from the fire swayed in time with the song. The blue streaks within the dancing flames looked like people for a moment.

A furious crash of thunder rolled overhead, and she closed her eyes again. She listened past the howling rain and the crackle of the fire. In the distance, she thought she heard a voice soft and beautiful singing the song, but with words she'd never heard before.

> *"Oh come, oh come, my child fair,*
> *I held so long ago.*
> *My court of magic and of light,*
> *Lies through the bitter snow.*
> *Sing with me, my dear sweet child,*
> *And for all time I'll keep you."*

The storm quieted, as if it had been driven back from the mouth of the cave. Wynn felt warm. The warmth started on the top of her head and spread down through her body the way honey spreads through water. She took a deep breath, her chest feeling less constricted by fear as she waited in the darkness.

The melody of the song hung in the air, floating over her like a mother's lullaby. They would find the Silver Gate. She knew they would.

"Wynn, wake up." Elric shook her shoulder urgently. "I told you to tend the fire, not fall asleep."

Wynn blinked her eyes open slowly, shielding them with her arm as she squinted at her brother. Her mouth watered. That's when she noticed the smell.

The savory scent of roasted meat filled the small cave, and Wynn sat up. Her clothes were still wet, but not terribly so, and the chill had gone, except for a bit on her back. Elric hunched over the fire, turning several sticks skewered through chunks of sizzling lamb.

"Oh! Oh!" Wynn clapped and waved her hands in front of her. It smelled so good. Her tummy pinched, then growled. Elric pulled one of the sticks off the fire and handed it to her.

Wynn tasted it and burned her tongue, but that didn't matter. She took a bite and chewed. She ate and she ate. Her jaw hurt from the effort of chewing, but she didn't care. She had never tasted anything better.

Elric flopped next to her and lifted one of the sticks, but didn't bite into it right away. He bowed his head and looked sad. The cuffs of his tunic were stained dark red. He took a bite and chewed slowly. It took a long time for them to eat. It always took Wynn a long time to eat because her mouth moved slowly. She didn't know why Elric was so quiet. Finally he spoke.

"You did a good job on the fire. I'm sorry it took me so long to return," he said, poking the healthy flames with a stick to stoke them higher.

"The Grendel came," Wynn said. "He tried to blow it out, but I didn't let him. But the Fairy Queen drove him away."

"That must have been quite a dream," he said.

"It wasn't a dream," she said, wiping her hands on her leggings.

Elric ignored her. "I believe the village that old man told us about is near. If we're careful and lucky, we may be able to stay in the woods. I can build us a hut here in the fells, and we can trade at the market. We can live by ourselves like Osmund does." Elric stared out at the distant hilltops and mountains. He looked thoughtful as he helped Mildred preen her feathers with his fingers. She shook them out, sending several little tufts of fluff into the air. One caught on his lip.

He fought to get the tiny feather out of his mouth. When he finally got it on his hand, it stuck to his finger and he couldn't shake it off. Wynn touched his knee to be sure she had his attention. Elric looked at her. "We are going to the Silver Gate," she said.

"Wynn, we have to be real now." Elric flicked the feather off his finger, only to have Mildred shake out her wings again and send new ones flying. He waved his hand in front of his face to keep them away. "Our best chance at survival is to find the village."

"The Silver Gate is real." Wynn wrapped her drying cloak around her legs. "I heard the Fairy Queen singing. She knows me."

"You were asleep." Elric gave her a look she'd seen many times before. The one he used when he thought she was being foolish. "You were even snoring."

"No, it is *real*." She knew what she saw in the shadows. She didn't fall asleep until after she heard the Fairy Queen sing. "She wants me to come to her."

"Wynn, think about it. Why would an all-powerful Fairy Queen, who has an entire realm of magical people to wait on her and do her bidding, pay attention to one girl sleeping in a cave?" Elric asked.

"She likes me." Wynn crossed her arms. "Osmund said she is sad. I could help to make her happy."

Elric rubbed his forehead. "Wynn, you are very good at being happy, but sometimes it is safer to stay with what we know," he explained. "Don't you want a home again? I will build us a hut like Mother's. Mildred can hatch chicks in the garden. You can gather sticks for me and tend to the weeds. I'll provide for us. We can't keep running off into the wilderness and expect to survive. We're starving out here."

"I'm not hungry."

Elric uttered a long growling sound that reminded Wynn of the times he pretended to be the Grendel. He took a deep breath and let it out slowly.

"Can you trust me to do what is right for us?" he asked.

Wynn thought about it. The Silver Gate was real. She knew she heard the Fairy Queen. But sometimes when she was right, it didn't matter. She still didn't get to decide.

Wynn sighed. "I trust you."

Elric poked the fire with one of the sticks. "Good. We'll find the village in the morning. This time, promise me you will stay near me and you won't speak. We have a better chance of staying if people don't notice that you're different."

A heavy feeling pressed down on Wynn. If they lived near the village, Wynn would have to stay inside again and not talk to anyone. She would have only Mildred to talk to if Elric was out working in the fields.

"Do you promise?" Elric insisted.

Wynn remembered the last time they visited a market. She didn't want him to be hurt again. She knew that was her fault, but she didn't know why. "I promise," she mumbled.

Elric kicked his feet up on a rock near the fire and leaned back against the slope of the cave wall. "Don't worry. Things will be back to normal before long."

Wynn frowned. That thought made her sad.

CHAPTER TWENTY-ONE

Elric

THE NEXT MORNING, WATER DRIPPED from the edge of the overhang, though the air was still, and the sky overcast. Elric hitched the sack up on his shoulder. "Stay close, and we have to be careful." He kept his ax in hand as they crept slowly down the path toward the place where he had seen the felled tree. Someone had to be nearby. They were near the village. He knew it.

With warm rain falling on the icy ground during the night, the mist rose, creating thick tendrils of fog that shrouded the world in a soft gray veil. The woods sounded unnaturally silent.

Wynn didn't say a word as she clung to his free hand and walked beside him. Not even twigs falling from the skeletal branches of the trees made sound as they hit the loamy forest floor.

"Hello!" Elric called as a creeping chill slithered down his neck. The air smelled damp and clean without the tinge of wood smoke. They walked on, the ground constantly sloping downward. A narrow path led down the hill and through the thinning woods. The mist grew thicker as the trees became sparse and they found themselves on a small rise.

"A lake of air," Wynn said as she pushed her ragged hair out of her eyes.

Elric turned, and to his shock, a lake stretched out before them. The mist lingered low over the water, making the lake seem as if it had been filled with clouds. The mist churned like a river current, driven by a wind he could not feel. It was as if the quiet breath of the lake itself moved the swirling mist.

"It's only fog," Elric said as he started off down the rocky path. But fog hardly ever lingered through the day like this, in spring no less. He wiped the back of his neck. The fog clung to his skin, leaving a crawling feeling all over him.

Wynn took a minute before she followed. He could hear her singing the song under her breath, the mist on the lake dancing to the haunting notes of the softly whispered tune.

> *"My queen, my queen, though road be long,*
> *And touched with bitter cold.*
> *On mountain white, in argent grove*
> *With leaves of shining gold.*
> *Please grant to me your silver branch,*
> *And through the gate I'll find you."*

"We have to find the grove now," she stated. "That is the way."

"Wynn, enough!" Elric shouted, his voice carrying over the still air. It winged across the lake. "We can't keep feeding this fantasy. It is getting out of control. Fairies aren't real. There is no Silver Gate. This village is our only hope."

Wynn blinked at him. "Father said I was from the fairies . . . a changeling."

"Why do you listen to what Father said? Father wanted to sell you as a slave!" As soon as the words left his mouth, the burn of his anger flushed through his body and he turned from her to hide all the things he felt.

"What did you saying?" Wynn asked. It was a familiar phrase. One she used to say hundreds of times as she tried to learn to speak. Clearly she was upset. Well, she had every right to be.

"He sold you to work in the lord's manor, where you would have had to beg for whatever bones fell from the table like a dog, be forced to sleep on the floor, and be beaten any time you did something wrong. That is why we had to run. So he wouldn't find you and take you away from me." Elric's voice cracked as he said it. "I couldn't let him take you."

Wynn turned from him, hugging herself, her thick thumb stroking her shoulder. "No one likes me."

He slowly turned to face her, feeling a burning tingle in the inner corners of his eyes. "I like you."

"You yell." She cast her eyes down and walked away.

"I don't mean to."

She gave him a skeptical look.

"It's just hard when you don't listen to me," he admitted.

"I listen. *You* don't listen. The Fairy Queen is *real*,"

Wynn said. "She sings."

"Your mind hears things." Elric adjusted the strap cutting into his shoulder and started off down the road. "What you heard is your thoughts that you made up."

"No." Wynn skipped ahead as if she had no understanding of the significance of what he was trying to teach her.

"Fine," Elric said as the pot in his sack clanged with each step he took. "The Fairy Queen likes to hear you sing. I hear you. That isn't going to change the fact that our only hope of survival is this village. Maybe once we are settled, we can look for the gate in summertime, when the weather isn't so treacherous. Will that make you happy?"

"The road to the Silver Gate is cold. Summer is warm." Wynn joined him by his side, clinging to the strap of her sack. She brushed her hair out of her face with a swipe of her palm.

Elric let out a heavy sigh. "Village first? Please?" Now he was resorting to the shortened phrases he had once used when she was smaller and only understood certain things.

She gave him a skeptical frown, but followed him humming the slightly off-key notes as the melody drifted through the thick fog.

The heavy mist grew thicker with each tentative step down the hill. Mildred's soft clucking from inside the sack punctured the ominous silence.

Elric saw something in the distance. Shadows that formed dark mounds in neat rows. Nature didn't create such forms. The village! His heart stuttered as he pulled Wynn forward. They'd found it. Finally, they would have a home. The grazing wasn't bad up through the forest. He could raise sheep again, and Wynn could tend a garden. There were plenty of trees. He could figure out a way to build a sturdy hut, and he could hide his sister away from anyone who would wish her harm. This would be perfect. But the air was heavy and dark, and the sky remained an iron gray.

Elric's unsettled feeling grew as they came nearer and nearer to the worn buildings of the village. It was quiet. Unnaturally so. He should have heard the sounds of animals moving through the streets, or peddlers calling out wares. A village on a lake should have had fishermen pulling in nets and haggling with fishmongers on the distant pier.

Instead there was nothing, not even the dire caw of a carrion crow.

Something was wrong.

"Stay close," Elric whispered as they came into the shadows of the dark wood buildings. Wynn pressed to his side, holding tight to his elbow.

"This place is bad," Wynn whispered.

Elric swallowed a hard lump of fear that had wedged in his throat. "Something terrible must have happened here."

"Where are the people?" Wynn asked.

"I don't know."

Row after row, the houses stood empty. It was as if everyone in the village had simply disappeared. They pushed on the door of the first house they came to.

"Is anyone here?" Elric called.

The door swung open with a groan that lingered in the stillness. A tangle of weeds surrounded the house, taking over neat rows of new spring vegetables and herbs sprouting in the garden along its side. Someone had to have planted them not long ago, but hadn't tended the garden since.

"Elric?" Wynn clutched his hand tighter.

Bones stuck out of the soft earth near the garden. It wasn't a bone pile, but a skeleton of small predator, a fox or a cat perhaps.

"The Grendel was here," Wynn said with a shaky voice.

"That's a story too." Elric peeked in the house.

Cobwebs and dust had settled over the meager belongings. An overturned pot waited near the fire, clearly untouched from the moment it rolled to the floor. A spider lurked in the center of a perfectly formed web across the mouth of the cauldron.

"The Grendel is real, he was in the storm." Wynn bumped into his side as she pushed close in the doorway.

"That was a dream." Elric said, taking another slow step inside the dim interior of the house. "Nobody seems to have been here for a while."

"I don't like this place." Wynn tucked herself closer to his side.

The door creaked again. Mildred poked her head out of Wynn's sack, then slowly pulled it back in with a wary *awwwwwwwwwwwk*.

A loud crack shattered the silence. Wynn screamed as she jumped around to Elric's front. A broom rested on the ground where it had fallen, knocked over by the door.

"Want to leave here," Wynn said, tugging on his hand.

Elric resisted her pulls and inspected the dim interior of the hut more closely. Perhaps there were things here they could use. A pallet of straw lay in the corner of the hut, the blankets askew as if someone had gotten out of them very suddenly, then never put them right. They were tattered and moth-eaten, but might be salvageable.

It didn't look as if there was any food, but maybe there was a tucked-away cellar for root vegetables and such. It was too early in spring to forage anything from the garden.

An uneasy feeling settled in his stomach. Elric picked up the pot and the spider crawled across his hand. He let out a shout and whipped his wrist, sending the spider flying toward the old wooden planks covering a tiny window. The leather straps holding the shutters to the dark wood framing had been cracked with weather and age. The spider righted itself and tucked its dark body under one of the thick straps. Wynn stepped closer to the simple dirt hearth as Elric wiped the back of his hand down his tunic to rid himself of the crawling sensation there.

"Let's go," Elric said. "We can check the rest of the village. Someone has to be nearby." Wynn was right, there was something very wrong about this place, but it couldn't be the Grendel. Could it?

Wynn patted Mildred in her sack, then stooped under the low door frame and walked through the garden and into the road. Mildred let out a sharp squawk of alarm and struggled inside Wynn's sack. Wynn turned to pat the kicking lump in her bag, but froze when a low rumble of growls reached through the fog. Elric's heart thundered as his immediate thought was of an enormous man-eating monster, no matter how irrational that thought was.

"Elric?" Wynn scrambled behind him as he turned toward the sound.

Three rangy dogs stalked toward them with their heads low, their dark eyes fixed. One was shaggy, its fur matted and tanged with bits of briar and leaves. The other two had smooth, splotched coats that stretched thin over visible bones. It looked as if they hadn't eaten in months.

"Run!" Wynn pulled on the strap of his sack. "Run!" she screamed as the dogs rushed forward.

CHAPTER TWENTY-TWO

Elric

WYNN PUSHED ELRIC, BUT HE couldn't seem to make his feet move. His instinct was to pick up a rock and search for his sling, but when he reached behind him, he grasped the handle of his ax. She clung to his arm and dragged him back as he swung the ax in front of them. Wynn pulled him into the nearest house.

As they scrambled through the door, Elric kicked it shut. One of the dogs threw its body against the thin wood, barking and snarling. Elric could see its muzzle dripping foam in the gap between the weathered planks.

"Move the table!" he shouted at Wynn. "We have to block the door!"

The dogs scratched furiously at the warped and cracked wood, damaged by years of rain. Bits and pieces of the door splintered under the assault of the dogs' claws. The gaps grew wider, giving Eric a clear view of yellow snapping teeth. The dogs attacked the wood, gnawing and pulling on the weathered planks with their sharp teeth. The sound of their snarls and barks filled the small house. The door shuddered as one of the dogs threw its body against it. The force strained the rain-swollen wooden pegs holding the door together.

Wynn screamed.

Elric looked back over his shoulder at where she was staring. A withered skeleton lay on the bed, clothes hanging off the bones like eerie skin.

Elric tried to fight down his sense of panic. They were trapped in a house with a dead man and murderous dogs fighting to get in. He couldn't lose his head.

"It's naught but bones. Bones can't eat us. Get the table." Elric couldn't tear his eyes from the grinning skull, even as he felt the impact of the lunging dogs on the door.

Wynn's lips pressed together as her brow furrowed

in concentration, then she ran to the other side of the heavy oak table and used her back to push it to Elric. He let go of the door, threw himself over the table, and helped Wynn tip it up so the solid surface crashed onto its side, blocking the door with thick oak planks.

The dog managed to hold a broken chunk of door in its jaws as it viciously whipped its head side to side until the plank came free. It shoved its snout in the newly opened gap, but the oak table blocked it from pushing through. The dog jumped against it, reaching a paw in and scratching at the edge of the table.

Elric took Wynn's hand and backed toward the center of the room. She tucked herself behind him as he scanned the small house, looking for a means of escape.

Black mold rotted the thatching above them, and darkened the hardened daub walls between the supporting timbers. The air smelled damp and foul, like sickness and death. Fishing baskets, pots and things lay around the house in disarray, things knocked to the floor but not taken.

It was likely those dogs had been foraging through the houses, looking for food now that their masters were gone. He didn't want to think about what else they may have eaten.

The dog gave up trying to fit through the broken door. Elric could hear the other dogs growling and huffing as they paced along the front of the house.

"The Grendel, he ate him!" Wynn said, pointing at the bones.

"Nonsense. He's in his bed. He probably died of sickness in his sleep. A plague must have reached this village," Elric said. The shadow of death lingered all around them like a living thing. "We can't stay here. We have to escape before we end up just like him."

A small door led out of the back of the house into a garden. To his right was a single shuttered window. The wood on both the window and the back door looked even less sturdy than the front door. Neither would keep those dogs out for long, and they were out of tables.

Wynn stepped closer to the window. Something slammed against the shutters.

"Get back!" Elric stepped in front of his sister.

Wynn shrieked as part of the rotted wood broke away. The mangy gray dog snapped and tore at the planks. Its frothy saliva dripped from its jaws.

Hungry and desperate dogs were one thing; mad ones were another. They'd never get out of this alive if the dogs were infected. Elric swung his ax at the hole, but the impact crushed the sill, and the dog's paws soon emerged, scratching away the dried mud of the daub wall, exposing the woven wattle beneath, and opening the hole wider. Elric met the dog's black and feral gaze as its scarred muzzle drew back in a growl.

Wynn ran up next to him as he pulled his ax free from the wall. "Wynn, stay behind me."

She didn't listen. Instead she pushed forward toward the mongrel's snapping jaws. She threw something out of the hole. "There!" she shouted at the vicious dogs.

All three dogs fell back, writhing in a mass as they began fighting with each other.

"What did you do?" Elric hastily grabbed both sacks as she pulled him toward the back door.

"Dogs like bones." She pushed out of the door and ran in front of him.

Oh, Elric didn't want to think about that.

Mildred squawked as they raced between the rotting buildings toward the edge of the lake.

"A boat!" Wynn pointed toward the water, where a small fishing boat bobbed lazily, tied to a rickety dock that was missing several boards.

The boat was probably in disrepair and full of leaks. But if it stayed afloat long enough for them to push out into the water, they would have a better chance of escaping those dogs out on the lake. Mad dogs would avoid getting wet at all cost. The only thing that had stopped one from attacking his flock was when he had run the herd through a stream.

"Hurry!" he called. Wynn stumbled and Elric pulled her up as the dogs chased after them. Their sharp fangs flashed as the dogs barked and snapped. Elric picked up a rock and threw it, catching one of the mottled dogs right in the eye.

It let out a yelp and shook its head, but the others didn't pause their loping strides. The one he had struck with the rock recovered and joined the chase only a body's length behind the others.

Wynn reached the dock, but then froze as she teetered on the edge of the rotting plank beneath their feet.

"Jump!" Elric screamed at her.

She hesitated, swinging her arms to keep her balance. "Too far."

"No it's not, jump!" The dogs were coming up fast.

"Need your hands," Wynn protested.

Elric grasped an old fishing net lying near the edge of the dock and hauled it up out of the water. Long trails of green muck clung to the ropes. "Go now!" Elric screamed.

Wynn swung her arms and jumped, letting out a sharp cry of fear as she landed on the planks on the other side. One of them broke beneath her, sending her foot through the dock and into the black water. She pulled herself forward to keep herself from falling in.

Elric threw the net, tangling the dogs as they thrashed under the rotting ropes. They fought and snapped, tearing at the thick net.

Elric leaped over the gap in the dock, tugged Wynn up, and pushed her toward the boat. She scrambled into it as Elric grasped an old split oar from the edge of the dock.

One of the dogs freed itself from the net and lunged.

Elric swung the oar, catching the beast across the face and sending it flying sideways into the shallows of the lake. It yelped as it hit the water and furiously swam back to the shore. Elric jumped into the leaky boat and used the oar to push them off away from the dock.

The mange-covered gray one jumped up onto the planks, but paced on the edge of the boards, unwilling to jump into the ice-cold water.

With his head pounding and his heart somewhere

near his ears, Elric paddled the small boat out toward the center of the lake. His hands shook and his breath burned in his throat. A small pool of water sat in the bottom of the boat. Hopefully it was a puddle from the recent storm and not a leak, but he couldn't count on such luck. He looked over at his sister.

"Wynn, are you hurt?"

She shook her head, not saying anything as she carefully opened the top of the sack. Mildred poked her head out, and Wynn tucked her safely back in.

"We're not hurt."

He swung his sack around to the seat next to her. He didn't have to tell her what to do. She pulled out the little pot and scooped up the water, throwing it over the side with a soft splash.

The mist floating above the surface of the water swallowed the sight of the dogs on the dock, but not the sound of their barking as it chased them across the lake.

"Elric?" Wynn's voice sounded shaky.

"What is it?" he asked, swinging the oar to the other side of the boat and sliding it through the water.

"I don't think I like dogs anymore." She paused her bailing for a moment to pat her sack. "Chickens are much nicer. They don't have teeth."

Elric let out a chuckle. He couldn't help it. He took several slow breaths through his nose in an attempt to calm his racing heart. Wynn methodically bailed out the boat, as if the dog attack had never happened. Sometimes he really loved having his sister around. She certainly kept him from lingering on bad thoughts.

"What do we do now?" Wynn asked, pouring another small scoop of water into the misty lake. "The Grendel is following us."

"We continue on," he said, without acknowledging her fears about otherworldly monsters. Elric paddled steadily as the fog enveloped them. Whether it was a monster, or terrible luck, danger did seem to follow on their heels.

CHAPTER TWENTY-THREE
Wynn

WYNN SCOOPED WATER OUT OF the boat and poured it back into the lake. She had never ridden in a boat before, but she knew water shouldn't be inside it, so she kept scooping it out while Elric paddled.

Mildred perched on her knee. She looked sleepy after everything that happened with the dogs. Elric did not look sleepy. He looked worried as he scanned the fog.

"I think I see something. Hopefully we didn't go in a circle," he said, squinting at the mist.

"We didn't," Wynn said. She knew it. They were

going the right way. They found the hands holding the moon, and the rain of stars, and then they crossed the clouds and found the lake of air. Tomorrow she would find the grove that the song talked about, and then they would be very close. It was the last step before they found the gate.

"Let me handle the directions. I know how to keep us on track," Elric said. The paddle made a splash in the water.

Wynn didn't respond. He didn't want to listen to her, she could tell, but it didn't really matter if he did or not. The queen wanted to sing with her. She said so in the cave. The queen would help them find the right way. Wynn peered out into the fog. "Trees!"

She could see them sticking up like black teeth on the foggy shore.

Elric paddled the boat until Wynn could see grassy lake weeds reaching up under the boat in the dark water. Elric leaned over and touched the paddle to the bottom of the lake, and he used it to push them forward. He picked up Mildred and threw her into the air toward the shore. Mildred flapped her wings and flopped onto the pebbles. She ran into the dried grass with her wings beating at her sides as she jogged over the rocks.

"Jump in. Go find some sticks and I can start us a fire," Elric said as he pushed them forward again. Wynn nodded, pleased that she knew what to do.

"Pick up sticks, pick up sticks," she sang to herself, the way she had before mother died. She heard Elric chuckle. Something tickled around her ankle. She leaned over. There was a string around her foot. She pulled on it. A grooved stone bauble was tied to it, and a ball of the string was wrapped around a curved bone handle, but the end caught on something.

"Wynn, what are you doing? Get to the shore so I can land this boat." Elric sounded grumpy, but she didn't want to let go of the string. She wanted to know how it was caught. Bending far over, she peered under the seat. A hook was stuck in the wood. She tried to hold it tightly with her short thumb. It was very difficult. She had to concentrate.

"Is something wrong?" Elric asked.

She got it! Wynn sat back up holding the hook tightly in her fingers. "Look!"

"A fishing line!" Elric's face looked as if a bunch of new chicks had hatched in the garden. "This is wonderful. We can fish tonight!"

Wynn was very excited that he was excited, but then

she felt sad. "I don't know how to fish. Water is danger. Mother said no."

He leaned closer to her. "Don't worry. I can teach you. C'mon, we have to dig up some worms."

Wynn was so excited, she wanted to start right now. She jumped into the water with a big splash.

"Wynn! You're going to scare the fish!" Elric laughed as he said it.

"I'm sorry," she said, lifting the shortened hem of her former kirtle. She was up to her waist in the lake. The water was cool, but warmer than she thought it should be after winter. The underwater grasses tangled around her legs, but she pulled out of them, then jumped a couple more times to see her feet splash.

Elric hopped out of the boat, sinking into the water up to his thighs. He pushed the boat up onto the shore. "The first rule of fishing." He held up his first finger. "Fish don't like noise. Or things splashing in the water. We'll have to wait for them to settle. Let's start a fire, then get those worms."

She leaned to the side and slapped the water at him. It splashed the side of his face. If the fish were already scared, they wouldn't mind a little more splashing.

"Hey!" His eyes went wide, but then he showed her

his playful grin and bent low. He slapped the water harder than she had, and Wynn squealed and ducked as the spray splattered over her back.

Her wet hair stuck to her cheeks, and she kicked water at him, but he used both his arms to push a big plume of water into the air so it arched like the tail of the rooster.

"Do you yield?" he taunted.

She shook her head, stuck out her tongue, and blew through her lips until she made a wet, farty sort of noise at him, then ran from the water onto the shore. "I won't yield!" she shouted with her hands on her hips.

Elric laughed, shaking out his wet hair. "Fine, I give up. We've got work to do before we start fishing."

Wynn did a good job gathering sticks. Soon Elric had a fire going on the rocky edge of the lake, and the sun peeked through the lifting mist.

The swell of hope surrounded her heart and squeezed. They were close to the mountain. Wynn could see the white peak over the tops of the trees. She wanted to talk about it with Elric, but he didn't seem to want to listen, so she thought about it instead.

Soon she would find the grove, and then the gate. They would be safe again, and Elric could return to the way he was before, when they were home. She missed the brother who smiled and was happy to see her when he returned from the field. Now he only worried about houses and villages. But fishing made him happy, and she wanted to catch a fish.

She set off along the shore of the lake, with Mildred at her heels. She turned over rocks, and plucked out several creepy bugs and worms, then placed them in the pot for safekeeping. She would have found more, but Mildred ate about half of them as soon as she flipped the rock.

Once she had lots of creepy-crawlies in the pot, she showed it to Elric.

"Good work!" He took the pot and peered into it. "You've got some young Mayflies in here too."

Wynn gave him a puzzled look. "Flies, they swim?"

"These ones are little; they don't have wings yet. The fish really like them." He pointed to the leggy things that Mildred liked the best.

Elric took the pot of bugs and the fishing line she had found, and walked over to a flat stretch of sand on the edge of the lake. He poked through the pot and set some of the worms and other bugs on the hook, then turned to her. "I'll toss the line, but you can hold it. If you feel something tug on it, yank it hard, then wind up the line."

Wind up the line? She looked down at the spool of line in her hand. This would be harder than she thought. If she didn't catch a fish, Elric would be disappointed. They needed the food.

"You fish," she said.

Elric placed the spool of line in her hand. "You can do it." He gave her a reassuring smile, then straightened her cap. She nodded to him.

"Stand back, I don't want to catch you with this hook." Wynn backed away quickly toward the trees. He let out a long tangle of line, then swung the little stone weight before sending the hook and weight flinging over the water. He beckoned for her to come forward, and she moved next to him with hesitant steps. With his arms around her, he showed her how to hold the spool of line and use her other hand to hold the thread, so she could feel if something bit at the hook.

"Remember, if you feel anything, grab the line and tug hard. Then wind it up, the way you would yarn," he explained.

Mother never let her wind yarn, either. But she didn't want to say that.

She could feel her heart pounding fast and hard. She watched the line on her finger, expecting to feel a twitch at any moment. But it didn't come. Elric went to go sit on a large rock. He whistled to himself. He didn't seem very worried that she didn't have a fish yet.

So she didn't worry either. But her arm got tired. Wynn drew in a deep breath and ignored the shaky, burning feeling in her arm. Elric said to hold it up, and she would. She wouldn't let him down. She really wanted to eat fish tonight.

That's when she felt it—a sharp tug. Wynn squealed. She forgot what to do!

"That's it! Bring it in!" Elric yelled. She tugged hard on the line, and the line tugged back. It almost pulled the spool out of her hand. She gripped it with both hands, but then she couldn't wind the line. She didn't know what to do! She couldn't make her thoughts move her hands that fast.

"Wind the line! Get it on the bank!" Elric shouted as he jumped down off the rock and ran toward her.

The line pulled and pulled. Wynn panicked. Holding the line close to her chest, she turned toward the trees and ran as fast as she could.

"What are you doing? You're not supposed to run,"

Elric called, but she kept going. She could still feel the tugging. Elric shouted in surprise, and then she heard a loud splash.

Oh no! She turned back around.

Elric had fallen on his backside in the shallows, a large bronze-colored fish flopping in his lap. He desperately tried to keep hold of it as it thrashed and flailed against him. Wynn pulled on the line, and the fish landed on the beach.

Her brother leaped out of the water and onto the fish. "I got it!" he screamed. But the fish wiggled out from between his arms. It didn't seem to be on the line anymore, and now it was flopping closer to the water.

That was her fish!

Wynn ran toward the fish and threw herself into the sand, grabbing the fish by the tail and holding on tight as it flung itself about.

"You got it! Keep hold." Elric ran out of the lake to dive into the sand beside her. He helped hold her hands tight on the fish's tail. It was a heavy, fat sort of fish with orange-brown scales. "That's the biggest bream I've ever seen! Not bad for your first try. A little unusual method." He winked at her. "But I'm so proud of you. Let's get this fish on the fire."

Suddenly Wynn felt as if the warmth of the fire came from her insides. This is what it was like to be proud.

An hour later, Wynn wiggled her toes as steam rose off the wet leather of her shoes. Her belly was full of fresh fish and another of Mildred's eggs. She was so happy. Fires were nice. Elric was good at making them. She watched the light flicker over his face. He had wrinkles in his brow that shouldn't be there, but he looked content.

"Maybe we can make it after all," he murmured, before he wrapped his cloak around himself and fell to sleep. Wynn watched the moonlight shine on the swirling mist above the lake.

She tucked her cloak closer to her body, and Mildred settled in her arm. They would make it to the gate. There was nothing stopping them now.

Wynn woke up at the first light and shivered. A fine frost coated everything, even her cloak. It almost made the ground look covered in snow. Mildred slept on her nest in the sack, her beak buried in the feathers on her chest.

The fire had gone out. She needed to find more sticks. Elric looked happy sleeping. She pulled his cloak closer to his neck, then set out into the woods to hunt for twigs to start the embers burning again. That would be easier than lighting it from the start.

Wynn kept her eyes on the ground before her feet so she wouldn't miss any sticks. She carefully lined up the skinny ones that wouldn't be good for burning on the path so she could follow them back to Elric.

She twisted through the bare branches of shrubs and little saplings growing through the blanket of leaves on the forest floor. As she glanced up, she noticed a path, and followed it toward a hill. The frost crunched under her feet as she walked, gathering the dry sticks as she went.

The first touch of sunlight warmed her face. She heard a rustle ahead and looked up.

A brown hare munched on some new spring grass growing in an open clearing on the edge of a large birch grove. The white bark of the trees shone bright in the new sunlight as the frost glittered silver on the ground. The trees were budding bright yellow leaves for spring. With the new sunlight behind them, they glowed gold.

Silver and gold. She was here. She found it.

Wynn hummed the song under her breath, thinking the words, hoping she could hear the voices sing with her again. Maybe this wasn't the place. It was beautiful, with the silver frost covering the birches, but it didn't feel magical. The woods were silent, except for the quiet munching of the hare. His ears turned forward and back as he ate the new shoots of grass.

Suddenly a young fox emerged from the bright white trunks of the birch grove. He lowered his head, slinking forward, pressing his golden-red body close to the ground. His fine black ears pricked forward.

He pounced, jumping straight up, his tail high as he landed in front of the rabbit.

Wynn held her breath, but to her surprise the rabbit reared up and danced on his back feet as he pawed at the fox in return.

The fox smiled, lowering in another bow, his tongue hanging out as he grinned at the mad spring hare. The hare fell back down on his paws, and both the rabbit and the fox bounced around the small clearing as if they were playing.

Wynn laughed at them, then sang the song to see if they would dance with the music the way the birds had done. The fox popped up again, bounding through the clearing as he pranced and pounced. The rabbit answered in kind, hopping delicately on his back toes as he pawed at the air and leaped around the fox.

Wynn watched the natural enemies dance to her tune, and she sang louder until laughter bubbled up into her voice. This was magical. The hare and the fox leaped and played. They were very good dancers. Maybe all foxes and rabbits should try to be friends. The light glittered around the animals, catching in the frost and turning it into a million points of sparkling light as a soft breeze fluttered through the new spring leaves of the birches.

"Wynn!" She turned at the sound of Elric's voice. He marched up the path with both sacks swung over his shoulder and Mildred on his heels.

"Here!" she called, wanting to show him what she had just seen, but when she turned back, the fox and the hare had gone.

"What were you doing up here?" he asked, breathing heavily. He had been running.

"I have sticks," she said, dropping her bundle at her feet. "For the fire."

"You did a good job, but I already put it out." He lifted his hand to shade his eyes, scowling at the birches. "This looks like a well-traveled path. Hopefully it will lead to another hamlet or village."

Wynn smiled but didn't say anything. She knew this

road would lead right to the court of the Fairy Queen, where the woods were filled with light and color, and the animals danced together as friends.

"Come on." She took her brother's hand. "Let's go."

CHAPTER TWENTY-FOUR

Elric

THINGS WERE LOOKING UP. ELRIC grabbed a birch stick and peeled the bark as they walked along the path. There was a chill in the air, but summer was coming soon. They still had a little bit of meat, and he kept the fishing line. Hares would be waking from hibernation, easy to hunt, and they had a clear path under their feet.

Even Wynn seemed less stubborn as she happily trotted through the birches with Mildred chasing at her heels. Wynn would take an extra-large step, and Mildred would dart between her legs. Then Wynn would take another long step, and the hen would weave through her legs again. It became a game between them, and it made Elric smile.

He leaned on a walking stick he had picked up to watch them play. This path had to lead somewhere, and soon they would be able to find a place they could settle and live in peace.

He had a decently steady hand, and Mildred had thick, stiff feathers. Maybe he could become a fletcher and make arrows, or begin to learn a smithing trade. Working with a large fire would be nice on cool mornings such as this.

"Do you think I'd make a good smith?" Elric asked, tossing the peeled stick into the woods.

"What is that?" Wynn halted in the path ahead of him.

"Someone who makes swords, and knives, and other things with metal." Chains and tools wouldn't be as interesting as crafting armor and weapons, but it was part of the job.

"Knives are sharp, careful." Wynn bent to pick up a stick of her own, crowned with yellow leaves.

Elric stopped on the path. Those were their mother's words. Wynn had even mimicked the cadence of their mother's voice as she said them. He could see her in his mind, running to Wynn, to pull her away from the things that would harm her as she repeated the same phrases over and over so Wynn could learn.

Knives are sharp. . . . Fire is hot.

Those lessons should have been obvious. Wynn had to work so hard for any piece of information she gained, but they still found their way deep into Wynn's mind through patience and effort.

Each one was a victory, because every small thing Wynn ever learned came with tremendous effort.

How could he teach her all the rest that she would need to know?

That night Elric prodded the fire as he watched Wynn sleeping peacefully nearby. Tiny flakes of snow began to fall, and he adjusted his cloak over his shoulders to ward off the chill.

The sight of the flurries dancing through the light cast by the fire reminded him of a night much like this one. Wynn had been about four and couldn't talk yet. Mother had laid her down to sleep near the fire, then stood in the doorway of the hut, looking out into the darkness.

"Who do you watch for?" Elric had asked.

She folded her arms across her chest with a heavy sigh. Her long sandy hair fell in two braids over her shoulders as she contemplated the new snow. "It snows when the Fairy Queen feels lonely. If you watch closely, you might see her through the snow."

Elric laughed at her. "You're telling me stories. Father told me grown men don't listen to such things."

Mother smiled. "And you are a grown man now?"

"I am six!"

She chuckled. "A very grown man indeed."

She opened her arms, stretching the woven blanket she carried over her shoulders out like wings. He rushed into them, and her arms circled him, enveloping him in the warm comfort of the blanket and his mother's embrace. She kissed the top of his head. "I am glad I don't have to be lonely. I have you, and your sister."

Elric looked up into his mother's gray eyes, so much like Wynn's. "If the Fairy Queen is real, why haven't I seen her?"

His mother looked out at the falling snow. "You will see what you believe you see."

As a boy, he pondered those words for years. Sometimes while out in the fields tending the sheep, he sat alone in the night and told himself that he believed. It never made a difference.

Wynn was counting on him, and he had to do what was best and what was right for both of them. Trusting in fairy tales would not help them survive.

Wynn mumbled in her sleep and turned over, pulling the cloak from her body. It snapped Elric back into the moment. He stoked the fire, their tiny shield against the cold, then he tucked the cloak back around his sister.

Sometimes he wished he could see the world the way she did. But he couldn't. He never would. The snowflakes grew thicker, large clusters of puffy ice falling from the dark sky. He huddled deeper into his own cloak and drifted off to sleep as softly as the falling snow.

Elric woke with a start. A heaviness pressed over his body and his limbs went numb with cold. His breath rose in a fog around his face as he tried to blink the sleep out of his eyes, but his lashes were crusted together. All he could see was white.

A blanket of snow an inch-and-a-half thick lay over everything, and fat snowflakes were falling from the dark clouds overhead. The wind picked up, and he could have sworn he heard a distant howl on the wind. He turned to the white lump next to him.

"Wynn, wake up!" He pushed the heavy snow off his

cloak, grateful that the thick wool kept him fairly dry. They wouldn't remain that way for long. He struggled to his feet but stumbled and fell. Pain stabbed through his legs, and he couldn't balance on his numb feet. "We're in trouble, wake up!"

He had to brush off a thick blanket of snow to shake her shoulder. Thankfully she stirred, revealing Mildred tucked in her cloak, close to her chest. His relief felt like sinking his shivering body into a tub of hot water.

Mildred shook out her comb and blinked at him with an uncertain *awwwwk*. Wynn yawned and stretched her arm up, the snow falling off her cloak in heavy clumps. Several of the snowflakes landed on the ends of her cropped hair, then melted.

She blinked at the frosty-white grove.

"It's snowing!" A wide smile broke over her face as she scrambled to her feet, shaking off the rest of the snow and brushing off her cap. It fell around her, leaving a ring of disturbed snow at her feet. She twirled in the thick flurries laughing at the dancing snowflakes above her, then hugged Mildred tight. The hen kicked at the sudden embrace. "This is wonderful."

"This is a disaster." Elric wrapped his hand in the hem of his cloak and brushed aside the snow enough to gather their meager belongings. He shoved what he could back in the sacks, his fingertips feeling like they would shatter in the cold. "We can't see the road." His teeth chattered as he said the words, so he clenched them tight until his jaw ached. If he hadn't woken when he did, they might not have woken at all. Another hour, two? He wasn't sure how long it took to freeze to death, and he didn't want to find out. He cursed springtime and its mercurial weather under his breath. It didn't help that they were traveling north and into the mountains.

Wynn walked over to him and placed her hen near her feet. Mildred flopped onto the snow, then flapped and jumped, trying to pull her feet out of it. She squawked, clearly affronted that she had to touch the cold snow.

"I got you," he said to Mildred, who had flopped on her side with her feet curled tightly into her feathers. Elric picked her up and lifted her to his shoulder, where she could perch. Her feathers tickled his ear, and he tilted his head into her side in a vain attempt to warm his cheek. She cooed at him and preened his hair.

Wynn trotted over to a tree and shook it. She giggled as the snow fell from the branches, landing on her with a soft plop. With her cheeks flushed red from the cold, she smiled at him.

The road had to lead somewhere. They might be close to some form of shelter, but that path would take them up the mountain. If they went down, they might be able to get below the snow line. But then the storm could turn to freezing rain. That would be worse. Chances were greater that they could find someone else living on the edges of the lake. Lakes offered resources. Barren, snowy, mountainsides did not. "We have to get down off this mountain right now. We'll head back to the lake. There might be another fishing village nearby."

"No." Wynn backed away from him, her feet creating long furrows in the snow as she dragged them. "We are going the right way." She pointed into the birches.

"We can't climb into the snow. We'll freeze to death out here. We must find shelter." Elric tucked his hands under the pits of his arms in an attempt to warm them as he stumbled along a downhill path. Mildred jumped off his shoulder and returned to Wynn.

"The village is dead. There are dogs." Wynn marched the opposite direction. Her footprints left dark pockets that marred the pristine white. Mildred tried to hop from one to the next, flapping with urgency, but her wings couldn't lift her heavy body out of the snow. "I'm going this way."

"Wynnfrith!" Elric tried to hurry after her, but his foot slipped in the cold mud beneath the snow and he had to catch himself against a tree. "Stop right now. You need to listen!"

She shivered, pulling her cloak closer to her exposed neck. The short fringes of her hair pushed up around her face like a mane. "I will find the Silver Gate." Swinging her arms, she began to sing that song for the thousandth time.

Elric gripped the branch of the tree until he feared it would snap. "It doesn't exist!" Elric shouted. "It is only a story Mother made up to keep you happy."

Wynn spun around and yelled. Her words clearer than normal. "No. Mother said the Fairy Queen is real! She said I can see her."

Elric took a pair of careful steps toward Wynn. "She taught you songs when you were little because it helped you learn to speak. You had to repeat things over and over before you could learn words, and songs were easy to remember. None of that song is true. It is nothing more than a bit of entertainment some minstrel made up to earn a few coins at market."

"It is true. I will find the Silver Gate," Wynn said, concentrating hard on her words. She stopped speaking for a moment and waited, as if the words were near her tongue, but would not rest on it. Finally she said, "It is close."

Elric shook the snow from his hair and raised the hood of his cloak, his ears burning from the stinging cold. How was he ever going to convince her to come with him?

Wynn walked back toward him and took his hand. "We found the dancing smoke, the fire river, the hands, the lake, and the grove." She swept her other arm out at the stark white birches. "Why don't you see?"

Elric grabbed her elbow and led her back the way they had come. She yelped in shock and pulled against him. He trudged forward, dragging her behind him. He managed only a few steps before he stopped. He didn't have enough energy to fight. It was too cold. He had to appeal to her. It was the only way. "The *smoke* was a flock of birds. The fire was a reflection from the sun. The hands were nothing but a tree in the darkness. The lake was covered in fog. It held water, not air, and there is nothing special about this grove. All of these things are perfectly ordinary." He looked around at the fat flakes of snow falling through the drooping branches of the birches.

"Why?" Wynn pulled her arm from his frozen grasp.

"Why don't you see?"

"I don't believe in magic!" he shouted. "It's naught but tricks and distractions that jugglers perform for coins at market." He swung himself behind her and tried to push her forward with his hip and shoulder, but she leaned against him. His feet burned and he couldn't bend his toes. "There is no magical force that can change things just because you want it to."

"Magic is real." Wynn turned to the side, and he nearly fell forward into the snow. She trotted away from him and backed up so he couldn't grab her again. "I believe."

"What do you know?" Elric muttered. "You're a half—"

He stopped himself before he said the last word, but it sat on his tongue like poison.

Wit.

She stared at him with deep hurt in her eyes. It was the same look she had given him when he had cut her hair.

And his guilt sliced at him like a knife. He didn't mean it. "Wynn, I'm so sorry."

"I know things," she said, her lips set in a soft frown as if this hurt cut so deep, it had lost its sharp edge.

"I said I was sorry. I'm just—" He rubbed his neck, soothing the ache that lingered there from carrying the sack. "This hasn't been an easy journey, and I don't know how much longer we can last like this."

"Am I cursed?" Wynn looked out into the tangle of trees. Her voice sounded so resigned, as if she were telling him she was tall, or hungry.

Elric put his hand on her shoulder. "You are not cursed." He said the words, but even as he said them, he thought about the years of poor harvests that had plagued the village where they had lived ever since the year she was born, and the number of misfortunes that had befallen them on this journey.

"Father said I was cursed. Mother kept me, and that cursed her, too." She looked far off into the distance.

"You're not cursed. You just need to be more sensible. Curses aren't real either. If you continue to believe in things that aren't real, you'll only be disappointed." He let the sack fall to the ground. Somehow he had to wrestle Mildred into it without getting scratched. The hen was still flopping around in the snow. She ran as soon as he neared her.

"I don't know what that means," Wynn said. The chilling wind picked up, blowing the heavy snowflakes away from her face.

"It means you can't think something is real and have it be true. You can't think, 'Oh, here's a rock' and have that rock suddenly appear. And when you don't get what you want, you will feel hopeless and sad and we will be lost high on a mountain in a snowstorm, where we will likely die."

Wynn bent down, brushed some snow to the side, and picked up a rock the size of her fist. "Here is a rock."

"That's not the point! None of the rest of it is real. I don't believe in the Silver Gate. I don't believe in the Fairy Queen, or the Grendel, or magic, or any of it. I can't believe it and I won't believe it." He slapped the snow off his shoulders and turned from her. He sniffed; his nose was dripping from the cold, and the dry winter air made his eyes sting. "Live in your fantasy all you want. I don't care. Just please, please, listen to me. I'm trying to save us."

She placed her hand on his shoulder. He turned to her, and she tipped the rock into his palm.

"Believing is easy," she said. "Like wishing for eggs. Lighting a fire is hard. You can do that."

Something deep within him melted as he closed his

hand over the smooth stone. For a moment he wondered where it came from. There had to be a creek or a river nearby to tumble the rough edges off it.

"I can't believe," he admitted in a soft voice as he stroked his thumb over the surface of the stone. "If I believed in fairies, that would mean they switched you for another baby. It would mean you're not my sister."

CHAPTER TWENTY-FIVE
Wynn

WYNN SHIVERED AS SHE LOOKED up at Elric. His lips were purple. That was strange. They didn't usually look that way. He wasn't making sense. Maybe it was the cold confusing him.

"You're my brother. Mother is your mother too." Wynn grabbed the edges of her cloak and pulled them around her body. It made her a little warmer. Her toes felt funny, though. Snow was sticking to Elric's hair.

"But if you were taken by fairies, then Mother wasn't your mother." Elric started walking and Wynn followed.

Walking made her feel warmer.

"I know my mother." Wynn trotted forward and caught Mildred. She didn't run very fast. Maybe she wanted to be caught. Wynn cuddled her close to her chest, tucking the edges of her cloak around the hen. The snow stuck to her bony legs.

"I know you know who Mother is, but if you really are a *changeling*, then she is not your real mother and I am not your real brother." His face looked sad, and serious. "I don't believe that."

"I don't understand," she said slowly. She didn't like saying those words. Elric always got frustrated every time she did.

"If the fairies exist, then they stole a baby and took her away and left you in her place." Elric made several gestures with his hands, but they made less sense than his words.

"I don't know that baby," she said, still watching his hands. "Is she my sister?"

"Never mind." Elric pushed his hair back from his face. "You don't understand, and it doesn't matter." He turned slowly in a circle, peering through the white trees. "The road is this way. We should be able to find the lake from here, but I can't see it through the snow."

More snow floated around them. It was very pretty, and Wynn took Elric's hand. "I know things. You're my brother."

He gave her hand a squeeze.

She wasn't worried. They would find the Silver Gate soon. Wynn wanted to sing, but when she opened her mouth, her teeth chattered, so she shut them tight and walked with Elric.

It wouldn't take long, and something would come to lead her on the right path. Then she could protect Elric and take him someplace warm.

But they walked for hours. They kept climbing so Elric could try to find a lookout and see the lake, but they didn't find one. And everything through the trees was a blur of white and gray. Still they climbed. Elric had wrapped extra cloth around her head. She didn't like having it over her mouth, but it was warmer with it on, so she didn't complain. She could feel her breath against the fabric every time she breathed out, warm, then cold and damp.

The snow was getting deeper. She couldn't pick up her feet as easily as she had before. Wynn tried to step in the pockets that Elric's feet made. Her ankles ached and she couldn't feel her toes.

But there would be a sign soon. There had to be.

The storm grew darker. Wynn's tummy rumbled and her body shook all over. She was cold, so very cold. There was a howl in the air.

Oh no, the Grendel was coming.

"We should be able to see the lake from here," Elric muttered, his voice muffled by the cloth tied around his face.

All Wynn could see was swirling snowflakes all around them. The silver trees had thinned out, leaving nothing but snow and rocks before them.

Mildred's head drooped. Her eyes closed as her neck fell limp against her breast.

"Elric!" Wynn called, tucking the hen closer to her body.

Mildred shouldn't look that way. That's not how she looked when she was sleeping.

Elric stumbled in the snow as he tried to come back to reach her. The wind picked up.

Cold cut straight through Wynn's body. She felt it like knives.

There had to be a sign. She just had to wait. But the Grendel would come with the wind.

"Get in the shadow of that boulder!" Elric called.

"We have to wait out the storm!"

A large rock jutted up out of the mountainside with a scraggly dead tree growing out from beside it. Snow drifted to either side of the boulder, creating a pocket of shallow snow right behind. They could hide from the Grendel there.

Wynn pushed forward, her heart racing as she clung to Mildred. "Don't worry, Mildred. We will be safe."

Wynn climbed, her feet slipping in the snow as she struggled to the rock.

Elric pushed her up from behind, and she collapsed in the shallow pit that the drifting snow had formed at the base of the boulder.

She stroked Mildred's feathers. Again she tried to sing, but her throat was too tight. She couldn't do it.

Elric crouched next to her and spread his own cloak over hers. He tucked her close to his side.

Wynn looked out at the dizzy swirl of falling snow, and a heaviness stole over her.

"Don't worry, Wynn. We'll make it through this." Elric rubbed her shoulder, but she could feel his body shaking beside her.

She didn't know if she could speak.

She wanted to close her eyes. She was so sleepy.

On the night of the storm, Mother wanted to sleep. Wynn kept trying to wake her, but she said she had to sleep. Sleep wasn't what took her, death did.

Wynn couldn't stop it. She tried to keep her eyes open, but they were so heavy. She didn't want to leave Elric alone. It would make him sad. He wouldn't have Mother anymore, and he wouldn't have her. He would be left with Father, who was angry. Wynn feared Elric would turn angry too. She didn't want that.

She was sad. She wanted to meet the Fairy Queen. Elric had said she was very beautiful. Wynn hoped she would be kind.

But now they would not find her.

"Elric?" she whispered.

"What is it?" He rubbed more vigorously, as if the motion of his arm could coax life back into her body.

"You are a good brother." She reached down and clutched her severed braid still tucked in her belt. He protected her. He always did his best.

He let out a huff, a half laugh. "I don't know about that." He pulled her in close to his body. "But I'm glad you're my sister."

"Thank you," she whispered. She closed her eyes. She could still see the bright light with them shut. "For taking me on an adventure. I'm sorry we didn't find the gate."

"Wynn?" She felt his hands on both her shoulders. He shook her, her head flopping. She couldn't keep it straight. She didn't want to anymore. Her arm relaxed and Mildred slipped out of her grasp. "Wynn! Don't go to sleep!"

The cold rushed in. She couldn't fight the storm anymore.

"I love you, big brother." Her words drifted far away from her on the howling wind.

CHAPTER TWENTY-SIX
Elric

"WYNN!" ELRIC PULLED HER TIGHTER in his arms, slapping her cheeks with his frozen fingers. Her skin looked blue. "Wynn, you have to wake up. Don't go to sleep. Please."

Mildred lay in the snow near Wynn's lap. She feebly flapped a wing. Elric grabbed the sack near his side and tucked the hen in it. Hopefully she would warm up inside. He didn't want to lose her, either. Wynn would never forgive him if she died.

With Mildred stowed away, Elric used both his arms

to lift Wynn closer to his body. The snow settled on the woven cap Osmund had given her and stuck to the frozen tips of her hair.

A desperation seized him, something primal and terrifying. He couldn't let her die here. Not like this. Not after everything they had gone through.

He wouldn't fail her.

"Wake up," he said to her. Her head lolled against his shoulder. His hands shook as he brushed a strand of her frozen hair away from her discolored lips. She was so still. Too still. A snowflake settled on her eyelash, but it did not stir. "You are the most stubborn girl I know. Don't you give up on me now. You never give up on anything."

He rocked her, but the motion did little to comfort either one of them. "You didn't give up when you had to carry me to that clearing. You didn't give up when you tried to mend Mother's spoon." He could feel the end of it poking into his back through the sack. Her patch hadn't held, but he didn't care. She had tried. "Wynn, you're a dragon. Fight. Please!"

Her eyelids fluttered, but did not open. Still, the slight movement gave him hope. He had to get her off this mountain.

He struggled to lift her to her feet, but his own legs were weak. He managed to drag her up to his waist, but her arms were limp. He shook so badly he couldn't hold her, and she fell backward into the snow.

She lay there, her limbs tangled around her and snow coating her cloak. It dusted every part of her, as if attempting to swallow her beneath its merciless drifts.

No . . . not Wynn. He couldn't lose her, too.

"Help me!" Elric screamed into the howling winds. They only grew louder and more monstrous. "Someone help my sister!"

The words ripped from his burning throat. He fell to his knees, unable to stand. "Help me, please."

Warm tears slipped over his cheeks as he pulled Wynn close and held her as tight as he could.

"I'm sorry." His tears fell onto her face. "All I wanted was to keep you safe. I didn't want to see you hurt. You didn't deserve it. You don't deserve this."

He gulped, his voice raw as his strength drained from his body. "I love you, Wynn. I'm sorry I couldn't protect you."

This was the end.

Elric let out a ragged breath, tucking his cheek against his little sister's head. She never stopped believing they would find a way out of this world that wanted to hurt them, that her song would save them.

Softly, so softly, he sang.

"My queen, my queen, I'll travel far,
To seek your favor high.
On mountain cold, with icy peak,
My road, it will draw nigh.
Please grant to me your silver branch,
And through the gate I'll find you."

His voice wavered, but as he sang, the winds stilled. He could almost hear music carried on the wind. Perhaps the storm was breaking. He didn't know where the words came from, he knew only that he had to finish the song. Without thinking, new words formed, ones Wynn never uttered in the thousands of times he had heard her sing.

"My queen, my queen, I sing for you,
Your audience I seek.
In your mercy, spare her life,
A humble servant meek.
Please grant to me your silver branch,
And through the gate I'll find you."

A loud crack shattered the sound of the winds as a branch the size of a large staff fell from the dead tree only inches from him. Ice coated it, giving it a silver sheen.

It couldn't be. This was impossible.

But hope, impossible hope, flared in his heart.

How could he believe what he was seeing?

You will see what you believe you see.

He heard his mother's voice as clearly as if she were standing beside him. As he looked out into the swirling snow, it parted, the snowflakes weaving and swirling together to create an archway before him.

Believing is easy. Wynn's voice in his memory sounded so matter-of-fact, as if her words were the simplest of truths. Perhaps they were.

Grasping the silver branch, he hauled his body upright. The strange, swirling gap in the storm gathered more and more snow on its edges, the arch becoming clearer.

Gritting his teeth, Elric shouldered the sack with Mildred, letting it sag beneath his arm, but left the other behind. He could feel his strength waning, and the gate shouldn't be far. The ice on the branch melted beneath the heat of his palm, but he gripped it tighter, clinging to the solid weight of it as he bent and hauled his sister up onto his back.

"I see it, Wynn," he murmured to her as he staggered under her limp weight. He settled her as he would an injured lamb on his shoulder. "You were right. We found it. Don't give up now."

He prayed the light of life was still in her. He was almost there.

He took one step, his foot dragging through the snow as he leaned on the staff, but he staggered and fell hard to his knee.

No. He would not give up. He could see it. He would make it to the gate.

"Don't give up." His words strengthened him as he pushed hard on the branch to rise again. "Don't give up."

One foot . . . another . . .

His body screamed at him in pain. He didn't care. It was nothing compared to the pain of Wynn fading before his eyes.

One more step . . . again. . . .

The bitter wind blew through him to his bones, stealing his strength, and begging him to lie down and sleep. *No.*

The wind died at the edge of the gate, though he

could hear it howling with rage just beyond.

He stumbled, falling forward into the snow with Wynn a heavy weight on his back. He was almost there. He tried to push himself up, to stand again, but he couldn't.

His eyes watered, and with his vision blurred, he swore he saw the arches of the gate solidify from the snow, a tower of ice and swirling mist. Light danced to the strange music on the wind within the depths of the ice. It was beautiful. The gate was only feet away. He could see a light now, like a glowing watery mist, a promise of life between the icy columns. The gate looked solid, real. For the first time, whether it was actually real or not didn't matter. It was right there. He *believed* it was real.

Throwing his arm forward, he used the branch to drag their bodies through the deep snow. He closed his eyes and shouted as he pulled. He was slipping, falling, tumbling into nothingness.

CHAPTER TWENTY-SEVEN
Elric

WARMTH SPREAD THROUGH ELRIC'S BODY. He was dead. It was over. Then suddenly pain flared through his limbs. His muscles ached and his hands and feet felt like they were on fire. Perhaps he wasn't dead after all. He didn't think being dead was supposed to hurt this much. His head seemed as if it were stuffed with thick wool. He blinked open his eyes.

A pair of enormous amber eyes blinked back at him only inches from his face.

"Arrrrrggggghhhh!" Elric shouted as he sat up

and scrambled backward. Soft moss felt like a sponge beneath his hands as strange blinking lights floated around his head.

He shook his head to clear his vision and looked upon the strangest creature he had ever seen.

About the size of a large cat, it had an elfish face and a mop of black hair. Its nose was long and pointed, and its teeth looked sharp and fang-like. Two enormous fox ears with deep-red tips pointed in different directions as the creature sniffed at him.

The top of its shoulders and arms were bare, though dark red fur grew over its forearms to the knuckles of its bony hands. The rest of its body resembled something like a rabbit coated with the same red fur. Instead of a fluffy white tail, a long ratlike tail that ended in a black tuft of fur swished back and forth as the thing stared at him.

It reminded him of an unfortunate mix of man and squirrel, and moved with the same twitchy energy.

"You are awake!" The creature had a strange high-pitched voice that didn't seem to belong to man or woman. It hopped around in a small circle, using its hands the same way an animal would use its front legs, then sprang onto Elric's chest and clapped. "This is pleasing, yes."

Elric used the side of his arm to swipe the strange creature off his chest. "What are you?" he asked. He glanced around. He appeared to be on a grassy bluff. The sky overhead shimmered with streaks and swirls of colored light. He'd never seen anything like it. But there were holes in the dome of light, dark places where the sky looked gray and storming in the distance. He pushed himself up and walked to the edge of the cliff. Just beyond the veil of shimmering color, a dark forest stretched out for miles, and beyond that, he could see the edge of a rocky and barren wasteland. Black clouds were building in that far and desolate place, a storm on the horizon.

Small mothlike creatures fluttered around him. They emitted light, glowing from time to time, turning bright red before fading back to white. "What is this place?" Elric added.

The creature slapped its strange tail on the ground and grinned. "I am Hob, and you are lucky. It is not easy for those from the Otherworld to find the Between. You fell and landed hard. *Crunch*." The strange beast demonstrated the impact with a loud slap of his hands. He hopped up and down with excitement. "Otherworldlings never come here. The queen doesn't have enough magic to make the gate appear anymore." He pointed to one of the holes in the sky. "But you did it! You made the magic."

Elric winced as he flexed his fingers. He shooed some of the glowing moths from around his head. "I must be dreaming." Hob bounced over to Elric's sack and began rummaging through it, the entire top half of the creature disappearing into the satchel. "Hey! Get out of there," Elric called, snatching the sack away, but not before Hob came away with the broken spoon.

"Ooooooh." The creature's large amber eyes glowed as he held the pot, then put it on his head like a hat. "Otherworld things." The pot nearly covered the creature's whole body. He hopped out from under it, then sat on it like a stool. He scrunched up his nose as he sniffed the handle of the spoon, then licked it.

"Give that back!" Elric snatched it away, and the creature's ears tipped down, giving it a sullen expression. It was pitiful, really, and Elric didn't wish to be rude. "Here, have the cork for the honey." He twisted the cork out of the top of the empty honey bottle and tossed it at Hob. He leaped high into the air and caught it, then bounced around Elric doing a flip every third hop or so.

"Oh, I likes you." He held up the cork and admired it before giving it a cautious lick. "I likes Otherworld creatures, and Otherworld things." He stared up at Elric with those luminous eyes. "I think I'll keep you, yes."

"We don't need all that," Elric said as he lifted the sack. Being "kept" by a bouncy and twitchy little creature was not on his list of things to do. Elric hastily shoved the spoon in the sack, when he noticed something missing.

"Mildred?" He glanced around but did not see the hen within the clearing. "Millie-lee-lee-lee!" he called.

Hob laughed again, a strange little cackle. "Do you call the Otherworld girl, or the feathered one? If you want the one with the beak, she will not leave the Otherworld child's side."

"Wynn?" Elric's heart threatened to pound out of his chest. "Where is she?"

"She fell over there." He pointed toward some dark trees climbing up the hill to his right. "Near the edge of the Darkling Woods. Strange creatures live there." He smiled, and the sharp points of his teeth gleamed. "Some are not so nice." His voice took on a growling purr that gave it a sinister edge.

Elric grabbed his knife and ran down the hill toward

the dark woods beyond the veil of shimmering light.

"Wynn!" He skidded to a halt, afraid to pass through the veil. The woods on the other side were bathed in shadow. The spaces between the trees seemed to move with unseen creatures. He imagined the glint of wary eyes catching the light of the shimmering dome that stood between him and the wood. There were holes in the shield above him. There must be holes near the ground as well, spaces where the dark creatures of the woods could creep through the fractured light. "Wynn! Where are you?" he called.

"Elric!" Wynn ran toward him up the hill. She limped, then stumbled, falling to her knees. Mildred stopped and waited for her to get to her feet. Elric did not wait. He ran for his sister and wrapped her in a tight hug. He was so glad to see her alive, so very glad she was with him.

"We did it," Wynn said against his shoulder.

"Yeah." He pushed her back just enough that he could see her face. He pushed her chopped-off hair away from her cheek. "We did it."

Her bright blue eyes looked up at him with a deep understanding shining in them. "You saved me from the snow," she said.

"No." He took her hand and pulled them both to their feet. "You did. You were right. I should have listened to you. I never would have found the gate if it had not been for you." Mildred hopped up and down beside them, flapping her wings as she let out a chorus of clucks. "Or you, Millie." He lifted the hen onto his shoulder, only to notice another bouncing creature at his side.

"And me!" Hob exclaimed, still clinging to his cork. "I am a great help."

Elric scowled at him. "I only just met you."

"Hello." Wynn turned and greeted the fairy creature. "What is your name?"

"I am Hob," he greeted with a toothy smile.

"I am Wynnfrith," Wynn said, her words slow and practiced. "Do you know the Fairy Queen?"

Hob immediately dropped to the ground and did not bounce up again. His fox-like ears folded down over the back of his head. His amber eyes shifted as he fiddled with his cork. "The queen lives in the great palace at the heart of this place. She is very ill. Her magic is breaking."

"Can you take us to her?" Elric asked.

Hob's eyes shifted over to the dark woods, then back to his cork. His whiplike tail thrashed behind him. "It is a long way."

Wynn touched the creature on the shoulder and his tail immediately fell still. "Please?" she said.

Hob looked up at her, one ear twitching back and forth. "I can't," he said, slowly turning the cork over in his hands. Thunder rumbled in the distance like an angry growl. Hob ducked down as if afraid of something, then glanced warily from side to side. "I can show you the way. Hurry. He is coming." He beckoned with his bony fingers, then hopped away from the woods toward a deep rolling valley in a patchwork of gold and emerald hills.

"Who is coming?" Elric asked, looking behind him. The dark clouds had rolled over the forest and were beginning to touch the edges of the swirling dome above them.

"He!" Hob shouted. "You must hide."

Wynn looked up at the clouds. "The Grendel."

Hob squeaked, and cowered behind her.

Suddenly the sound of thundering hooves echoed off the hills. Wynn tucked herself close to Elric's side. Two pure-white stags appeared out of thin air, galloping toward them. Elric threw himself in front of Wynn to shield her from the charging beasts. They stopped short, holding their silver antlers low so that Elric could see the colored lights from above reflected in the mirrorlike surface of the sharpened points.

Hob let out a wild sort of howl and sped off through the grasses toward the dark woods behind them. One of the stags raised his head, then leaped after Hob. He gave chase until the little creature slipped through a hole in the veil of light and disappeared into the dark woods beyond.

Elric had turned to watch the stag chase Hob. When he turned back around, a tall man with white robes and a silver trident stood where the stag had been. His glowing red eyes flashed. "Who are you? Where did you come from? And what business did you have with a darkling creature?"

CHAPTER TWENTY-EIGHT
Wynn

WYNN PEEKED OUT FROM BEHIND Elric. This man was a fairy. He could change into a stag. This was amazing! She stepped around Elric. "I am Wynnfrith," she announced.

"Wynn, no," Elric said in a hushed voice, grabbing her by the arm. She didn't let him pull her back.

"We came through the Silver Gate. We want to see the Fairy Queen." Wynn smiled at the man, knowing he would take her to the castle.

"Wynnfrith of the Otherworld?" The tall man took

a step back and bowed. His eyes changed from red to a bright green. "The queen has been expecting you for a long time." He pointed his trident toward the center of the valley where a great tree grew, with spires of glittering stone surrounding it. It looked like a castle. "Come, we must hurry before the Grendel reaches us."

In a flash of light, the man became a stag once more and charged forward along a path that wound through the hills. Wynn followed him, and Elric fell into step behind her. He carried Mildred, who clucked in amazement as she cocked her head to look around.

It was very colorful here. Even the grass seemed brighter than it ever did in the woods at home. The sky was filled with colors that swirled and shifted above them. She could see clouds through patches in the light. Flowers grew through the grasses, creating blankets of pink, white, yellow, and lavender across the land. The forests bloomed with flowers even though the leaves burned bright with the gold and red of fall. Wynn couldn't see a shadow anywhere. Except the clouds were coming closer. She didn't want the Grendel to catch her. So she ran.

Animals of all sorts flew or crawled out from the woods and grasses heading for the great tree. They were probably people too, just like the stag, and they were afraid. The queen would protect them; Wynn knew she would. She still had magic.

Elric stepped closer to her and looked back over his shoulder at the storm. "Wynn, I want you to let me talk to these people when we reach the palace. We have to be careful."

Wynn straightened and stood as tall as she could. "I said things to the stag. He's taking us to the queen."

"Yes, but we have brought trouble in our wake, and if you say the wrong—"

"I won't hide." Wynn stopped. She wasn't afraid of the coming storm. "I hid with Mother. I won't hide."

The stag bellowed at them. Elric nodded to her, then turned to jog forward. "Be careful," he said.

Wynn's chest felt full of warmth as she ran past him. "I will."

He stayed at her back, but didn't say anything else.

Finally they reached the great tree. Wynn wasn't sure she should call it a tree. It towered above them, taller than a giant. Its great branches scraped the sky as the pillars of rock soared to the clouds. They formed a perfect circle, ringing the tree. Wynn thought she could see people walking along the branches above, but it was so far away, and the light of the sky was so bright here, she couldn't trust her eyes.

They passed between two of the stone pillars, and entered a courtyard. Great rocks were carved with symbols that glowed blue, forming rings to their right and left. Wynn could feel a charged energy in the air. The storm was gathering, held at bay by the light surrounding them.

A gap in the great tree's roots created an arched doorway. Gold wove through the ropelike fibers of the wood, framing the open door. The stag changed into a man again, who greeted two guards at the door with a sharp nod.

Their eyes flared red as they looked at her, but Wynn held Mildred close and didn't tuck her chin or move behind Elric this time. They entered the biggest room Wynn had ever seen. Light streamed down from somewhere above them. It was like there was no ceiling, but there was no sky, either. The space felt too big for her, and at the same time, safely cocooned. Wynn crossed the circles etched into the smooth stone floor in the pattern of a flower with three petals and approached a bed on a platform in the center of the room. Behind it, a large, clear crystal floated in the air like an enormous shard of ice. An ugly crack cut through the heart of it, nearly severing it in two. Beneath the crystal was the silver bed. It looked as if it were made of ice, and softly falling snow swirled around it.

Everyone in the room fell still.

Mildred let out an uneasy cluck, and Wynn stroked her head to comfort her.

A woman sat up on the bed and looked toward them.

She was just as Elric had said. Her skin was dark brown, like the richest earth in the garden. Her snow-white hair floated around her face like a soft cloud. A crown of ice and burning flame adorned her brow, and she wore a dress spun of frozen dew on spiderwebs. Her eyes glowed blue, then the brightest of sunny yellow as she looked at them both.

"Wynnfrith, dear child." Her voice echoed through the chamber. "You found the way." She rose from her bed, and the guards in the room hissed in a sharp breath. She opened her arms and smiled.

Wynn placed Mildred on the ground and ran forward. She threw herself into the arms of the Fairy Queen. They closed around her in a warm embrace, and for the first time since her mother's death, Wynn felt safe. A bright white light surrounded them. It shone through her as it reached up toward the broken crystal. Wynn closed her eyes. "I am home."

CHAPTER TWENTY-NINE

Elric

ELRIC HAD TO SHIELD HIS eyes as a burst of bright white light emanated from the center of the crystal and flooded the large chamber. It shot skyward through the branches of the tree like a bolt of fiery lightning, and the energy of it made his hair stand on end. A cry of shock and elation rose up. Elric blinked as he looked around. The formerly empty chamber was now filled with people. Elric had never seen anything like them, their clothes, hair, faces. He had never seen so much color, and light played all around him as the tree itself glowed soft blue.

"She's well again. Her magic has returned," a woman with short bright-green hair said next to him. Her eyes glowed lavender as she spoke, her golden skin flushed with excitement. "We're safe once more."

Elric pushed through the sudden crowd and approached his sister. The Fairy Queen knelt down and smoothed Wynn's hair out of her face.

"I don't understand," he said. His thoughts were muddled and confused. It was as if visions from deep in his imagination had come to life. "I know you. I've seen you before."

The queen rose and faced him. "You did, many years ago." She walked toward Elric, still holding Wynn's hand. Mildred stepped out from behind him. The hen immediately bowed low, her beak touching the stone, and her wings spread out. Elric bowed as well. The queen reached out and touched his chin, lifting him back out of it. "You were only a baby yourself, still hiding behind your mother's skirts."

Elric desperately tried to remember what happened, certain that such a strange encounter would have imprinted itself on his memory forever. "There was snow."

"Yes." The queen drew her hand up in an elegant arc, and snow began to fall in thick, heavy flakes from somewhere high above them. The crowd pushed back toward the walls of the chamber, but Elric remained in the center of the room with the queen. "It was a cold night, and the snow fell that night because I had lost something precious to me. That's when I found her, a perfect baby in the snow."

"So you did take my sister. My real sister." Elric needed to understand.

"I stole no child," the queen said, her eyes flashing bright orange. The mist and ghostly snowflakes swirled around her in a sudden gust of wind.

"That can't be right. Wynn was born imperf—"

"Wynn was born as all in your world are born." The queen's words echoed in the chamber. "She is as she ever was, as she should be."

If what the queen said was true, that meant Wynn really was his sister. Mother was right to protect her, and so was he. For as much as that thought strengthened him, he was tormented by a hundred other questions still unanswered.

"But why is she different?" he asked.

"That is a question that does not need an answer. What can it change?" The queen took Wynn's hand and smiled down at her.

Nothing. It would change nothing.

Wynn smiled back, her expression wide open and adoring. She let go of the queen's hand and returned to him.

"I told you you're my brother." She bent and scooped up Mildred, who was lingering near his heel.

Elric turned to address the queen. "Then what happened that night? The night I saw you in the snow."

With a wave of her hand, the room grew dark and filled with swirling snow. The flakes of snow glowed with a ghostly light but did not feel cold as they landed on his cheeks. "As I said, I found a perfect baby in the snow." The queen's eyes changed to the pale and lonely color of ice. Just then a tiny cry floated through the chamber. It sounded distant, but there was no mistaking the baby's desperation. The queen looked down at the floor. The image of a baby appeared, created from soft light, mist, and the swirling snow. "She was not the first baby I have ever found abandoned. For many years I have taken in those children lost or left to die in the woods because they have been cast off by your unforgiving society, and I raised them here as my own. But Otherworld children do not change what they are, even here. They grow, they seek knowledge and answers, they do not remain children forever." She bowed her head and closed her eyes for the briefest of moments, as if she felt a sudden pain she wanted to hide. "This land is more eternal. Things do not change so easily here."

The queen bent down and lifted the squirming baby formed of snow and mist and cradled her in her arms. "I took the child I found in my arms. I looked into her eyes and kissed her fluffy dark hair. She had already nearly been covered in snow." The queen cradled the ghostly baby as if it were her own. The baby reached for her face. "I warmed her, I comforted her, and I sang to her."

Wynn let out a little gasp and clapped her hands over her mouth. Her eyes went wide.

The queen's changing eyes met his. "I loved her as if she were my own child in that moment, and that bond is not easily broken."

Elric's heart pounded so hard in his chest he thought he could feel it in his throat. His eyes stung as he watched the queen in the swirling magical snow. He understood.

The queen turned and waved her hand again, the ghostly baby still cradled in her arm. "I was about to leave the Otherworld, and take dear Wynn with me. But then I heard it."

Suddenly the room was filled with the wailing scream of a woman.

"No! Please, I beg you!"

The crowd circling them let out a cry of surprise and fear. Suddenly a woman, formed of mist and snow, ran forward toward the queen. She carried a toddler boy, her hair in a long braid, and her face painfully familiar.

"Mother!" Wynn called, and took a quick step toward the illusion. Elric threw out his arm and blocked her from moving forward. He needed to see this.

The ghostly woman had luminous tears streaking down her face. Slowly she put the toddler boy, him, on the snowy ground and held out her arms to the queen. "Please, she is my daughter. Don't take her from me."

The queen tucked the translucent blanket around the ghostly baby. "I told her I found the child abandoned. It was my right to claim what is left alone in the woods."

Mother shook her head as the ghost of Elric as a tiny child clung to her skirt. "Her father brought her here. He stole her from her basket. But she is mine. I love her, and I will protect her. Please don't take her from me. She is my heart."

The queen stepped close to the ghost of their mother and tipped her head to the side, as if lost in her own memory. "I still remember the look in her eyes. I knew how she felt. I too had a child stolen from me. Though a magic thread had already formed between me and this baby—Wynnfrith—I knew I could not allow another mother to suffer the pain that I had known." The queen held out the child and returned the baby Wynn to their mother's arms. The ghostly little boy stumbled forward in the snow and waved to the Fairy Queen. The queen gave the little boy a smile, then the spell was broken.

Light flooded the chamber, and Elric felt as if he had woken from a dream.

"But the decision to show mercy cost me greatly. My power has weakened in all the years since. Until now." The queen stood tall as a silence fell over the room. "Your mother promised me she would protect Wynn at all costs. And she did, until her last breath. She kept her promise to me. But that thread of magic between Wynnfrith and me was never broken, and I missed the child that should have been my own." She walked over to Wynn and conjured a perfect white rose, then handed it to her. "I have watched over you all this time."

The queen turned to Elric. "I feared there was no hope that you would find the gate. I feared you would not be able to see it, that you wouldn't pick up the staff. But you surprised me." Her eyes glowed green. "Your mother would be proud, and so am I."

The queen bowed to him, and suddenly everyone in the room fell to their knees before him.

Elric couldn't breathe. He was nothing more than a lowly shepherd and serf. No one had ever bowed to him, and he felt lost as he looked around the vast chamber. Wynn pushed close to his side and took his arm.

The queen rose and conjured a silver crown. She placed it on Elric's head, then turned and created another for Wynn.

"All hail Prince Elric and Princess Wynnfrith of the Otherworld." She held out her hands and addressed the people. "Let there be no corner of my realm that does not welcome them. Let this be your home."

A great cheer went up, and Wynn gave Elric a hug.

"You were right," he said to her as music filled the air around them. "You were right about everything, Wynn."

"I told you." She reached up and tipped the crown. "I wanted to be the dragon," she muttered.

Elric laughed as Mildred squawked and flapped her wings. He scooped up the hen and let her perch on his shoulder. She gave the crown a sharp peck, then fluffed her feathers near his ear. Elric's heart filled with warmth and light, and he knew this was joy.

The guards came forward. "My queen, the Grendel is retreating!"

The queen closed her eyes for the briefest moments, then opened them again, her expression serious and regal. Her changing eyes met his. "He will return," she said. "And when he does, my realm will need a hero, one who will not back away from his calling. You have shown great bravery and fortitude." She walked toward him and waved her hand through the air; as she did so, a sword appeared, formed from ice. It glowed flaming white, then revealed itself, forged in shining silver and crystal. "In the future, I hope that you will stand and protect this realm as you have protected your sister."

Elric knew what he had to do. He kneeled before the queen. She touched the sword to his shoulders. "Rise, Prince Elric."

He got to his feet, and Wynn pressed close to his side and took his hand.

"Our hopes rest with you," the queen proclaimed, and another great cheer filled the chamber.

"And me," Wynn added.

"And you," Elric agreed as he kept his sister close.

ACKNOWLEDGMENTS

I'D LIKE TO THANK MY family for their support and patience during the writing of this book. I could not do this without them, especially my husband, who supports me in so many little ways. If I ever didn't say thank you for all that you do, know that I am thankful for you every single moment we have together. The other person who is always there to shore me up through the good, the bad, and the why-did-I-write-that is my critique partner, Angie Fox. We've learned a lot from each other over the years, and I'm always grateful for her hard work and insight. I'd be lost without her.

I'd also like to thank my agent, Laura Bradford, for championing this project and always being a steady and guiding force in my career. I am grateful to my former editor, Anica Mrose Rissi, for believing in me, and I wish her all the best of luck on every new adventure she pursues. As for my current editor, Alexandra Arnold, I couldn't have asked for a brighter and more professional partner to work with. She helped shape this book into something special that I am very proud of. Thank you for bringing out the best in me.

During the writing of this book, I had the help of two very special editors who took on the daunting task of reading through my early draft and giving me their expert opinions on the story. Thank you to Sophia Wagner and Maddi Gwinner for your insightful observations and responses to the story.

I am humbled to be a part of the team at Katherine Tegen Books, and I appreciate all the hard work of everyone involved with my publisher. You all make magic happen, and I'm very grateful. I'd also like to give special thanks for my cover and the hard work of the designer, Aurora Parlagreco, and the illustrator, Lisa Perrin.

Finally I'd like to thank all the doctors, specialists, teachers, and therapists who dedicate themselves to working with very special kids. Thank you for everything you do, and all the love and kindness you give to those around you.